الكلمة الطيبة صدقة

هديت الى الدكتور الاستاذ الفاضل

علي نوري زادة

FROM BAGHDAD TO BEDLAM

حبيب لندن ٢٠١٩/٥/٣ م

From Baghdad to Bedlam

An Immigrant's Tale

Maged Kadar

with Noel d'Abo

SAQI

London San Francisco Beirut

Maged Kadar is married with two sons and lives in Kingston-on-Thames. He grew up in Al-Hay, southern Iraq and, after the rise of Saddam Hussein in 1979, fled to Liverpool where he met his wife. He went on to work as a cab driver in London and now teaches Arabic and Islamic Culture to British troops in Germany.

Noel d'Abo, former editor of *Period Homes* magazine, is now a full-time gardener in south London where he lives with his wife, two daughters and five cats.

ISBN: 978-0-86356-635-6

A full CIP record for this book is available from the British Library.
A full CIP record for this book is available from the Library of Congress.

Manufactured in Lebanon

SAQI
26 Westbourne Grove, London W2 5RH
825 Page Street, Suite 203, Berkeley, California 94710
Tabet Building, Mneimneh Street, Hamra, Beirut
www.saqibooks.com

Dedicated with love
to Carole
and our two sons,
Abbas and Jasim

Acknowledgements

I am eternally grateful to Noel d'Abo without whose help this book would have been impossible to complete.

I would like to thank Rebecca O'Connor, John Fisher of the Public Records Office, and the late Dr Zaki Badawi of the London Islamic College for their help; also Faz, Bill Bates, Selma Hanid and Alicia Brunicardi.

Civilisation has a darker side
Which must be accepted with the good.
The arts of sex and music, the art of might,
The art of being kind, the art of straightforwardness,
The art of deceit, the art of kingship,
Justice and the enduring crown ...
The resounding note of musical instrument,
Rejoicing of the heart, the kindling of strife,
The plundering of cities, the setting up of lamentation,
Fear, Pity, Terror.
All this is civilisation.
All this I give you,
And you must take it all with no argument and,
Once taken ... you cannot give it back.

Ishtar, Sumerian Goddess of Wisdom, *circa* 4000 BC

Foreword

It was all that time spent waiting for a fare in my clapped-out minicab that first got me writing.

Here I was, an Iraqi in London, living just off Portobello Road, married to a Liverpool girl and now the proud father of two sons. Yet instead of elation, all I felt was pain.

It was late summer of 1987, and Saddam's war with Iran was at its height. I was totally addicted to the daily news coverage of 'my' war and wrote to my family in Iraq to tell them of my despair:

In the name of God, the Compassionate, the Merciful.
Dear Family,
Woke up today on a typical British morning with all the muscular aches and pains any pilgrim to the Promised Land of Fog must suffer.
Today's symptoms are rather different, however, to those of Liverpool and the old Birkenhead Docks. We're in London now and the children are at school. Abbas is six and doing well.

9

I am teaching the children the Arabic alphabet and they want to learn about the Prophet Mohammed but their grandfather, Tommy, who's been here the last few weeks, keeps teaching them English swear-words instead.

The other day Jasim, who is now five, was standing on the balcony holding a balloon. Tommy told him to let go and watch it float up to heaven, because God might like one too!

When Carole's not shopping or taking tranquillizers, she cooks and cleans at the same time. She's very keen on bleach.

The house smells so much of it I have to keep my eyes closed, which means I'm getting plenty of sleep!

I'm wearing those thick cotton pyjamas you sent me, sitting on a carpeted floor waiting for the latest from the battlefront on the BBC's One O'Clock News. I never thought the war would last this long.

After seven years nobody here in England seems to care. Please forgive me for leaving you to face all this on your own. I'm always thinking of you and pray for this war to end so that I can bring Carole and the children to meet you …

Carefully, I folded the thin blue sheet of airmail paper then, running my tongue along its sweet gummed rim, glanced at Carole's picture resting on the window ledge.

There, beyond the large west-facing window of our fourth floor apartment I looked towards the BBC Television Centre in Wood Lane. The grandfather clock chimed one.

Time for my daily fix: the latest lunchtime news from Iraq, with Jan Leeming or John Tusa.

Today it was Jan who delivered the addictive hit I needed.

'The slaughter continues ... Iran attacks Baghdad with long-range missiles ... Iraq attacks the Kharg Island oil terminal.'

All these lives being lost – in terms of numbers, they seemed to have as much relevance to the world as the points scored in a basketball game.

At 1.15 each day, according to the clock in the hall, Carole would return from Portobello to find me glued to the screen.

Soon she'd be doing exactly the same, but with one important difference. In those distant days TV was all about war for me; for Carole it was all about soaps. No, not bleach, but *Sons and Daughters* first, then *Take The High Road*.

We were both going through so much pain. When apart we would pine, and when together, little would go right: a sure sign that all was well, probably.

It was early evening. Time for yet another night shift, but tonight I felt different, for tomorrow was our wedding anniversary: seven years since Carole and I married and seven years since the Iran-Iraq war began. Sadly, I still felt a stranger in my own home. What I longed for more than anything was for Carole to understand my Arab heritage.

Beyond the vacant stares of the trembling junkie, the hungry shoplifter or the sexless street girl, sunshine beamed above the horizon. Like long fingers, the sun's rays beckoned me towards them, and in a moment I was no longer a cab-driver parked somewhere in Little Venice, but a young boy back in al-Moraibi.

All is quiet, winter silence broken only by the lone cock crow. Frost-covered earth and puddles frozen over; morning mist clears revealing a small Arab village surrounded by lush green fields.

Dawn breaks, a reddish haze rising from darkness: no hills obstruct the view; just flat land as far as the eye can see. The arc of fire grows minute by minute, as bright red rays send warmth to the waking village.

The fiery circle is now complete: God Himself revealed in the sublime beauty of His creation, His brightness lighting up the sky, His omniscience filling the earth with all its bounty.

By noon, this silent panorama has transformed itself into a ghost-like haze as the sun-scorched earth is baked in waves of shimmering heat that float like wraiths before me.

I look up and see three eagles circling high above the plain in perfect formation. They scan the earth with unblinking gaze, the space between each unchanging.

I climb the chimney of the old kiln and peer far into the horizon beyond, to distant fields and secret places, dreaming I might glimpse that rarest of sights, the desert deer.

Focusing on a tree somewhere beyond, I imagine I possess the power to move that tree left, right, up or down, just as I please.

I can turn sand into water ... one blink, a desert then, suddenly, a huge sea: an ocean.

I can hear the waves and smell the tide, even now.

1

I was born in the village of al-Moraibi in 1957, the seventh son of eight children, all boys. The village lay just beyond al-Hay, a small town in southern Iraq dense with palms that grew thick by the River Gharraf.

I remember the *souk* and the scent of fresh herbs and spices, sounds of street traders hawking their wares while women, young and old, draped themselves in silks from the Orient and gems from the Gulf.

Our house was one of forty dotted along a half-mile stretch of river, part of the ancient canal system of Mesopotamia. The whitewashed single-storey building formed a square, a garden of lemon trees at its centre, surrounded by a courtyard paved with black and white marble tiles. Fringed on all sides by tall palms, the house stood alone on a river-bank where each winter we would catch fish in abundance from a little wooden bridge that linked us to the rest of the village.

In summer, the river would become so dry we'd stand at its

centre and pray for the return of winter and water. The air became so hot that it was painful to breathe and, by late afternoon, the wind was so strong it could almost lift you off your feet.

When evening came, we'd light oil lamps, a luxury unknown to the rest of the village.

There was a large rectangular building separated from the house called the *diwan*,[1] which seated about eighty people and was furnished throughout with locally woven rugs and carpets. It was here that the social life of not just our family, but almost the entire village was centred. When visitors were expected we would fix a lamp to the flag-pole above the *diwan* to guide them through the night. The light could be seen for miles, illuminating even the darkest sky. The oil lamp had a hypnotic effect, so much so that some guests would stare at the flame for hours.

One night a guest arrived late and was asked to turn off the lamp before going to sleep. Next morning, my brother walked in and found him in a terrible state.

'I didn't sleep a wink. I've spent all night trying to blow this lamp out!'

The lamp worked on a pump action; the harder you pumped, the brighter it illuminated a small mesh bulb, housed in a very thick glass casing.

The most treasured sight for my family, as well as for other villagers, was the green silk flag that flew above our *diwan* where, inside, on the wall, was a tapestry with the words 'The Living, The

---

1. Coffee reception room for entertaining guests. Sadly, the coffee ritual is now practised mainly in the countryside and viewed with disdain by most city Arabs in Iraq. The townies, who call themselves *hadhar*, 'civilised people', pride themselves on their ability to assimilate all things Western, referring to those who continue to carry the torch for their ancestors as uncivilised country cousins, *al-Arab*!

Everlasting',[1] embroidered in blue and green. The green of the flag signified the family's strict Islamic belief.

On the left side of the entrance to the *diwan* stood the *magsala*, a mobile three-in-one wash-basin built layer upon layer like a large wedding cake. Ours was fairly typical, consisting of three aluminium basins decorated with traditional Arab designs. The top section was the smallest for the soap; the next section, twice as big, contained enough fresh water to wash your face and hands, and beneath that was the largest tray, an overflow for waste water.

Some *magsalas* could have as many as five or six sections to complete a sanitation system, first introduced during the Abbasid era in the tenth century and, in some parts of Iraq, still in use to this day.

I remember my history teacher telling me a story about a mysterious group of Vikings who arrived on the shores of Mesopotamia and, according to Islamic custom, were to be washed and scrubbed before being presented to the Caliph of Baghdad.

A *magsala* was wheeled in but the Vikings were unimpressed. Their chief washed, then spat in the soap dish before urinating in the overflow; probably the first recorded misunderstanding between East and West.

The story goes that the horrified Caliph, disgusted by this infidel behaviour, ordered the Vikings to be taken away without further delay, adding an Islamic aside that, in some quarters, still holds water today: 'They are God's cattle on God's earth: feed them, then let them go.'

In the other corner of the *diwan*, just to the right of the

---

1. From the verse of al-Kursy, 'The Throne', the most reflective verse in the Qur'an. On display in most Muslim homes and places of work.

entrance where the brass coffee pots were neatly arranged in front of the fireplace, a large chimney-breast stuck out from the front of the building. The fire provided enough heat for both brewing the coffee and warming up any passer-by in the cold of winter. It was a common occurrence to walk into the *diwan* first thing in the morning to find a total stranger helping himself to a cup of black coffee after spending the night curled up on the carpet. Arab hospitality means that everyone is welcome: everyone is family, provided they respect local customs.

I remember finding a surprised guest in the *diwan* one winter's day. I had been woken by the sound of the cock crowing; nature's call for the whole village to rise and face a new day. After I had greeted the unannounced guest and exchanged a few words, he began to tell me of his journey, how tired and cold he was and his relief at having stumbled across our hospitality. He had been travelling for days and still had some way to go.

He introduced me to his passion: the female falcon. Continuing what seemed a rather unexciting story for an unenlightened ten-year-old of how he reared falcons and was in search of their eggs, I excused myself out of boredom and left. How I wish I'd stayed to hear more.

All I remember with clarity now was the stranger telling me that to really know a woman one must understand the ways and wiles of the female falcon first for, contrary to common belief, it is the female falcon who is the actual bird of prey, not the male. The male falcon is capable of catching a rat, a bat or a mouse at best; it is the female, however, who does the real damage. With a longer wingspan and more powerful muscle structure than the male, her intelligence and ambition are on a far higher plain. Rabbit, gazelle or even man himself is fair game for the female of the species.

My most vivid childhood memory is my *Khitan*.[1] I was six years old.

It was mid-morning when my father called me into the spare room, a room we normally used just for haircuts but, this time, I noticed a small branch no bigger than my middle finger lying on the table: it must have come from the lemon tree in the courtyard.

Next to the lemon branch, I saw a ball of cotton wool, bandages and some hand shears, and that's when sheer terror took over.

The operation is simple: anyone can do it. The foreskin is pulled forwards over the branch and then, once in position, the mullah[2] recites a short prayer, gives a sharp twist, a quick snip and it's all over. A few hours after snipped branch and foreskin fall to the ground the party begins: feasting followed by singing and dancing, then more feasting and dancing, all day and into the night.

While the mullah busied himself bandaging my wounded boyhood, my parents talked through my cries of pain assuring me that I was now a man; a man of worth, a man of substance.

I had sacrificed my own flesh and blood 'in the name of God'![3]

Somehow, in return, I expected God to relieve my pain immediately, but I was in such agony the following morning that I ran from the house over the bridge to the old kiln, where I tore off my blood-stained bandage and sat in the sand, legs apart, nursing my painful gender.

Normally, sand amidships is man's worst enemy but this time, it

---

1. Circumcision, a traditional rite of passage for all Muslim males.

2. One who is able to read and possibly write; knowledge is merely an option.

3. *In the name of God, the Compassionate, the Merciful*; the opening of every chapter in the Qur'an; also the prelude to every *halal*, or permissible act in Islamic life, whether washing, eating, slaughtering, travelling or making love.

was my greatest relief. I praised God and rejoined the celebrations, now into their second day, for my first proper meal since breakfast the previous day. Spit-roast lamb never tasted sweeter.

Another boyhood memory is the annual visit of the *Zejairis*, or Marsh Arabs, Iraq's ancient people; a living remnant of old Mesopotamia.

The Marsh Arabs came from the area where the Rivers Tigris and Euphrates meet, a wild and beautiful marshland; floating manmade islands in freshwater lagoons where they make a living fishing, raising water buffalo, cutting the reed-beds and cultivating the rich soil along the shore.

The inaccessibility of the marshes meant that their simple way of life remained virtually unchanged for thousands of years.

I would eagerly await their annual migration from the south each summer to al-Moraibi to help us bring in the harvest, before rejoining their families at the onset of winter and the fishing season.

One morning, I remember hearing a loud commotion from the fields where the Marsh Arabs were harvesting. We ran outside to see men, women and children running towards us, all screaming and shouting.

They were so upset, not even my father could calm them.

'Master, look up there!' they cried, 'The sky's breaking in two!'

As old and young alike threw themselves to the ground, I looked high into the blue beyond to a straight, white vapour trail that the Marsh Arabs believed was God Himself slowly, silently tearing their world apart.

2

As members of the two most prominent families in al-Kut, my parents married soon after the end of the Second World War in 1947.

My father's family, the Khedhirs, were known as Sayeds, descendants of the Prophet Mohammed, while on my mother's side, the al-Omara family prided themselves on never having allowed their daughters to marry outside the clan.[1]

What added spice to their union was that the Khedhirs had once owned the land surrounding al-Kut, but eventually lost it all, because they refused to cooperate with any foreign invader – the Turks before the Great War, then the British immediately after it.

The al-Omara, on the other hand, cooperated happily with both the Turks and the British and had been delighted to accept our

---

1. The only other occasion an outsider was allowed to marry a daughter of al-Omara was in 1953, when the late Crown Prince Abdul-Illah married Princess Hiyam, daughter of Sheikh al-Omara Mohammed al-Habib. It completed a circle of migration linking the last great Arab family to leave the peninsula for Iraq with the very first.

confiscated land: first, a huge chunk from the Turks in the nineteenth century, then the little that was left from the British in the 1920s.

As a result, the al-Omara family were now very rich and the Khedhir family very poor, but when my father asked for my mother's hand in marriage the chief of the al-Omara, Sheikh Mohammed al-Habib, who understood and respected my family's stand, gave his blessing.

It was the Khedhirs' first home win for generations.

From that moment on my father became a dedicated, religious man, an ascetic who expected nothing less from his children.

As the only literate adult in the village he would help with the spiritual and emotional needs of the villagers, as well as their general welfare; their education, tax affairs and wills. At evening classes, he would teach them how to read and write but, probably wisely, chose one of his students to teach us, his children.

I remember my father standing in prayer on a quiet summer's evening near the *diwan*, when the silence was suddenly broken by a fearful sound. A wolf was inside the sheep pen but, as the shepherd raised his rifle, my father, still deep in prayer, gestured not to shoot.

By the time he looked up again, the wolf was gone and with it, the lamb.

The shepherd was furious, unable to understand my father's logic in not wishing to kill the wolf there and then. My father simply smiled, 'The wolf, too, is God's creature doing God's will: like us, he must eat!'

My mother was far more practical about life, with a strong Islamic belief in destiny – whatever we do, or don't do, is decided well in advance. She would often say, 'It is all written on your forehead.'

When her father died, the local women came to pay their

respects, weeping and wailing and, at first, she joined them. The next thing we knew she was telling them to stop crying and start celebrating. After all, he had lived more than a hundred years and was still praying five times a day two days before he died!

Whenever facing a family crisis she would sit quietly reciting the Qur'an, before deciding the best way forward. For more difficult family decisions, however, she would use flour, ash and a wooden shuttle from her spinning wheel.

First, she would make the shape of a 'plus' sign on the kitchen table using flour for the horizontal line and ash for the vertical, then spin the shuttle and, if it came to rest along the white horizontal line, all would be well. If the shuttle hovered along the vertical black line this meant caution must be taken. She was happy, whatever the result.

Once, I made the mistake of blowing the flour and ash all over the kitchen floor mid-spin: she hit me hard across the back with a frying pan, reminding me never to abuse her flour arrangement again.

My mother's shuttle made its biggest mark the day my father ran into some Bedouin tribesmen just back from a camel raid in Kuwait.[1] There must have been about twenty of them, all tired, hungry and expecting lunch, but there was not enough flour or rice in the house to feed them so my father left his guests in the *diwan* while he asked my mother's advice.

Ushering him out of the kitchen, back towards the *diwan,* she told him firmly, '*Allah Kareem*.[2] Don't ask me, ask God! You'd

---

1. There is a rare breed of white camel, known as the 'Kuwaiti White', which has been the subject of a centuries-old dispute between Iraqi and Kuwaiti Bedouin tribes.

2. 'God is gracious'; Arabic equivalent to 'Don't worry!'

better go back to your bandits and pray for a miracle!'

As there was no flour in the village shop she went over to the barn with her shuttle and some ash, and then opened a sack of what she thought was building sand. She cut open the sack, hoping the sand would offer God's guidance but, instead of sand, out poured fresh flour.

My mother's prayers were answered, the camel raiders were fed, and my father managed to persuade them to stop their warlike ways.

'Allah be praised!' was a phrase I heard many times that day and, from then on, I would never again show disrespect for my mother.

3

I was eight years old when my grandfather told me the story of the Englishman who came to his house during the Great War.

It was 1915. My grandfather's shepherd had been called away to fight the Turks and another was needed quickly.

Out of the blue, a fair red-faced man introduced himself as a Kurd named Mohammed. My grandfather offered him the shepherd's job, which included three meals a day, a small house and coffee-making duties in the *diwan*, as and when required.

Mohammed accepted.

He would graze his flock from dawn till dusk, with lunch brought to him at noon, before returning to his quarters each evening to sleep. This same routine continued for months until, one day, a farm worker went to the fields to bring Mohammed his lunch but couldn't find him anywhere. The farmer searched and searched, calling out Mohammed's name, but to no avail. The shepherd was nowhere to be seen but then, suddenly, the farmer saw something glint in the sun behind some brushwood.

On hands and knees the farmer crawled quietly towards it, where strange sounds – rhythmic, but tuneless – could be heard coming from deep in the thicket.

He moved closer and there, crouched in front of him, was Mohammed the shepherd leaning over a wooden box. He was holding something to his ear, while tapping his finger on a one-note piano.

The shepherd looked up, startled.

The farmer was so frightened he dropped the *safer-tas*[1] containing the shepherd's lunch, and ran back to the village as fast as his legs would carry him to tell my grandfather what he had seen.

At nightfall, the shepherd returned to his quarters as usual but, instead of his sleeping rug, found a new mattress and pillow.

He asked my grandfather, 'Why have you put out a bed for me?'

'You are my guest.'

My grandfather then repeated the farmer's story about the *Engleez*[2] and invited the shepherd to eat with the family as his honoured guest. Mohammed the shepherd sat down and told my grandfather everything. He was an English army sergeant from Kent here in Iraq on a secret mission to help us win independence from the Turks so we might prosper once more.

At the next coffee meeting my grandfather introduced his British friend to the villagers and, from that moment on, the locals treated my grandfather's honoured guest as one of their own.

They even gave him a name: Mohammed al-Sarjoun.

Mohammed left the village the next day never to return, his mission complete.

---

1. A traveller's bowl; a series of food containers hooked together by a light aluminium frame.

2. Arabic word meaning 'the English'.

Soon after hearing my grandfather's story, I fell asleep and saw two British planes above a white strip of desert where nothing ever grew. The planes landed side by side, noses dipped like two hornets stinging their prey, planted two spiked spheres, like mines, neatly into the ground, then flew away.

I never forgot that dream, convinced that war between our two countries was inevitable unless Iraq and Engleze got to know each other better, like my grandfather and his soldier friend, al-Sarjoun.

By the time I was twelve my mind was made up: I would go to England to meet al-Sarjoun and ask to be his shepherd in Kent.

4

The art of hospitality is one of the great lessons that Arab parents teach their children from an early age and it is in the *diwan* that this tradition is most usually on view.

The tradition began almost two thousand years ago when Arabs discovered *qahwa*, coffee. Ever since, Arab culture has revolved around food, coffee and tea which, with liberal quantities of sugar, are the glue that binds the Arab world together.

The coffee culture began with *al-Mu'allaqat* (The Hangings), when Arab poets would meet in Mecca's Ukadh market square to read their poetry in public: the best-received work, often in praise of love, a local hero, or even a favourite horse or camel, was then displayed on the walls of al-Ka'ba.[1]

---

1. 'The Cube', Islam's holiest shrine. Believed to be built by the Prophet Ibrahim (Abraham) and his eldest son Ismael (Ishmael), father of the Arab race, and the one prepared for sacrifice by his father. The Qur'an also mentions Abraham's other son Isaac; and Isaac's son, Jacob, who became father of the Jewish race. According to the Judaeo-Christian tradition it was Abraham's second son, Isaac, who was sacrificed. The Qur'an, on the other hand, states clearly that it was Ishmael. However, all agree that the sacrifice was not made,

In those pre-Islamic days, visitors to Mecca would return home to discuss the merits of their favourite poem at coffee meetings far and wide throughout Arabia. Incredibly, seven original pre-Islamic 'hangings' still survive. For most Arabs since 610 AD, the pinnacle of the Arabic language is found in the Qur'an.[1]

In our village, coffee meetings in the *diwan* were an almost sacred ritual, where new visitors to the region would be welcomed and current affairs debated, from the local to the universal, often with religious or political overtones. It was a cocktail of authentic Arab culture and hospitality that, once tasted, could never be forgotten.

People would travel long distances for coffee in the *diwan*. Some would come on horseback, kitted out like knights, while the less privileged made their way on foot. A trickle of locals would wend their way towards our *diwan* as soon as they heard the sound of the *hawen*, the large coffee grinder, ringing out like a church bell.

---

as God was only testing Abraham's faith, and a sheep was sacrificed instead.

1. *Al-Qur'an* translates literally as *The Recital,* and it was the ability to read and write in a single language that first united the Arab peoples into one nation over a thousand years ago but, by the time I left Iraq, my father was one of only three in the entire region able to read or write, the other two being mullahs. The rest had assumed a social code based entirely on the oral tradition. The word 'mullah' derived from the verb *'imla'a'*, 'to dictate', a classic verb of the Arabic language, sadly unrecognised by most Arabs, not only as the root of the word 'mullah', but as the root of most of their problems today. In my village it meant the ability to dictate all kinds of written communications, including not just the Qur'an, but also letters from loved ones, tax orders, land deeds or whatever document was presented. Those unable to read were therefore, by implication, denied the ability to learn through the written word. Once the tradition of reading and learning was broken, the culture of dictatorship grew and grew until, quite unconsciously, we had drifted into two nations: the dictator and the dictated. As long as you had the school certificate or degree confirming your ability to read, you could become a mullah in your own right, an accredited dictator. Is it any wonder that dictatorship became a way of life, replacing Truth and Justice the original Islamic message demanded in the Qur'an?

My earliest memory of coffee is not just the scent or the taste, but the sound of coffee beans being ground in this copper container, so heavy only the strongest could lift it. When the coffee-maker's pestle struck the sides, the *hawen* rang out loud; a traditional message of welcome to any passer-by to join his fellows at the weekly coffee meeting.

At these meetings there was only one discipline that had to be observed: if we suspected guests hadn't eaten, rather than embarrass them by asking directly whether they were hungry, we would greet them as if it were morning and, if they replied with a morning response, we would feed them.

As soon as guests arrived, they'd start rolling their cigarettes, comparing taste and strength; even non-smokers got involved.

Then they'd compliment each other's ornate robes and beads and, if there was a new thoroughbred to admire, they'd leave the *diwan* for an inspection outside, where the owner would proudly show off his horse, the plaited reins, bridle and shining leather saddle finished in the finest silk embroidery.

This was just the start of the coffee meeting: an informal introduction, while the green, sweet, earth-scented coffee beans were roasted, ground, then filtered through a series of copper coffee-pots, each filtration poured into a smaller pot until the final brew was poured into the smallest and shiniest of them all.

Tradition demanded that once the coffee was ready, the coffee-maker select one of the guests to give his verdict on the hot, black, sugarless brew: attentive silence, a short sip, then a gentle shake of the china cup towards the host signified approval.

The coffee meeting could now begin.

Speeches could be about anything. They might be beautifully

rhymed, moving the crowd to cheers or tears, while some didn't go down well at all.

One coffee meeting I will never forget was hijacked by a Baʿath[1] Party official from al-Hay soon after Saddam took over Iraq in 1968. Before we knew what was happening, an entertaining cultural evening had turned into a lecture on socialism.

'Socialism is good for the village ... we must all share Iraq's wealth equally!' the party official bellowed.

A local named Asker leapt to his feet, keen to know more.

'What if my neighbour has two cars, and I have none?'

'You get one of your neighbour's!'

'That's a great idea! But what if I have two shirts and my neighbour has none?'

'He gets one of yours!'

'That's a lousy idea!'

Asker's brief flirtation with socialism had lasted less than a minute.

---

1. Baʿath Party: the Arab Baʿath Socialist Party, '*baʿath*' meaning renewal, or 'renaissance'. Established in Syria in 1947 by a local academic, Michel Aflaq, its doctrine propounds Arab unity based on socialist ideals but, since the formation of the State of Israel in 1948, has taken an increasingly anti-Western stance. By the mid-1960s support for the Baʿath Party had increased sufficiently for it to become the party of government in both Iraq and Syria.

5

Serious matters such as sex outside marriage were often debated at the weekly coffee meetings, and I well remember a villager named Azeem using the occasion to accuse another of raping his niece.

The object of his fury was not present, but 'that someone' would hear about it soon enough.

For committing deceit and creating calamity;
To you I say,
'Whoever should die first will be content.
Even if you reside beyond heaven and earth,
My reach is far.'
And who can object when I kill you?
If you say,
'But our line of kinship will be severed,'
To you I say,
'By the one we face five times a day,

I shall find a way.'
If you flee like a migrating bird,
To you I say,
'I shall be a hawk in the farthest sky.'
If you swim away like a fish in the deep,
To you I say,
'He who is soaking never fears the rain;
I shall come after you.'
If you dig a grave and bury yourself,
To you I say,
'I will come upon you
With the weight of the sky and the earth,
And I will fear neither spirits, nor man,
For they will never untangle you from my hands.'

It was Azeem's personal declaration of war.

One hot afternoon a few days later we heard what sounded like dogs barking and horses galloping somewhere in the distance. We went outside to look and there, through the dust, we could see men running – some on horseback with guns, others with swords and daggers glinting in the sun – chasing a single horseman heading straight towards us.

As he got closer, he leapt from his horse and dashed into the *diwan* just yards ahead of the pursuing mob, which gathered outside urging the man to surrender. The fugitive dusted himself down and asked for a jug of water, before hugging each of us one by one.

'They won't try anything here; not in your house … they wouldn't dare!'

This was Lamoud, a lovable rogue in his thirties, a highwayman. When there were no travellers to rob, he would steal livestock instead, then collect the reward for their safe return.

His parents thought he worked for a charity.

That night, Lamoud told us his story:

'I saw this beautiful girl one day while I was raiding her village to steal some sheep. There she was with her flock, so beautiful she made me lovesick.

'A few days later, I went back to her village and introduced myself.

'We talked and flirted, then found a hiding place behind some bushes where we could talk out of sight. We began to meet regularly. We fell in love.

'One night, unable to sleep at the thought of that soft skin like melting butter, that scent of henna and musk on her clothes, I could contain myself no longer.

'I arrived outside her village, tethered my horse and quietly made my way towards her house. After I woke her, we tiptoed to our hiding place in the fields and lay on the grass: I stroked her hair as she held my face, kissing and devouring me, and soon we were as one in paradise.

'Once our passion cooled, I realised the enormity of what we had done: we had committed a mortal sin. I had tainted her family's honour and now it would be impossible for her to marry a reputable suitor.

'I spoke of my fears for her future, but she seemed unconcerned. She had no regrets and suggested I go and lay low awhile. I told her I would do anything to marry her as soon as it could be arranged and no one need know what we had done, but she insisted her parents would never approve of me.

"What will you do?"

"For the honour of my family, and as one no longer pure, I must go away."

We kissed and parted and I never saw her again.

A few hours later, she had doused herself with petrol and given herself to God.'

Tears poured down Lamoud's face as he stood, head bowed, clutching his beads. Never had he imagined that a moment's passion could end in such tragedy.

Lamoud stayed with us for a few more days, while his accusers would come and go to check his whereabouts until, one day, he decided to reply to Azeem at the next coffee meeting.

The *diwan* was packed as Lamoud rose to his feet.

He asks, 'What of Guilt?'
To him I say,
'Guilt is the source of sorrow;
The avenging fiend
That follows me with whips and stings.'
He asks, 'What of Refuge?'
To him I say,
'The wildest beasts will hunt me from their dens
And birds of prey molest me in the grave.'
He asks, 'What of Remorse?'
To him I say,
'The wheel of passion now stands suddenly still
For, without repentance,
Remorse is the poison of life,

The echo of a lost virtue.
Yet Remorse is the first step
On that stoney path back to virtue.'
Finally, I ask,
'What of Forgiveness?'

Looking directly at his accuser, Lamoud tried to continue, stammering the word 'forgiveness' before breaking down.

Azeem crossed the *diwan* towards the trembling Lamoud, his arms outstretched.

'God will forgive you!' he shouted as the two men hugged and cried together, while everyone else shook hands with each other and thanked God for such an outcome.

By forgiving what seemed the unforgivable, Azeem ensured that his family name was immediately restored and that family honour would continue to be as important as life itself.

6

For man to kneel, then prostrate himself before God, as if embracing Mother Earth, is for the Muslim the most natural act in the world. Man's relationship with the earth is no different to the natural bond between mother and child for not only did God create man from earth through Adam; it is to the earth that man must ultimately return.

So, to the Muslim, prayer is an expression of thanks for the life God has given, and unquestioned surrender to the fate He has chosen; an act of kinship and devotion repeated five times each day ... for a lifetime.

Prayer works on the 'Practice makes Perfect' principle.

First, by standing upright before God, confirming His unity and Oneness, man's status in the natural order as the only creature in God's kingdom physically capable of standing before Him is proved.

In the second position, you bow with hands on knees, with words confirming God's greatness and mercy.

Finally, on both hands and knees, you prostrate yourself to the lowest level, the forehead, as one with the earth, man's ultimate submission before the Most High, before repeating again this physical and mental workout, recommended by God Himself, a total of seventeen times.

Prayer comes before everything but, despite this, not all God's messengers are welcome, even in al-Moraibi.

Mullah Mahmoud was a Muslim missionary from Iran. He usually arrived around June or July when the temperature was at its height but, unlike other mullahs who visited the region and knew about Islam, this mullah knew nothing.

We hated him.

Our first sighting of the mullah would be a bold, bright blob of colour, pink or yellow, appearing on the distant horizon. Then we'd see the mullah himself, fat and squat, slumped on his horse as he rode in from the east beneath a brightly coloured parasol, shielding him from the burning sun.

All the children looked forward to the visit of the man from the land of *Ajam*, Persia, but it was not his company, nor his personality that excited them. In fact, his presence guaranteed grief for almost all the adults in the village but, for the children, the prospect of his toys and sweets meant that they eyed the horizon longing for that first taste of his Persian delights. Chocolate, halva, pastries, and all types of rock were his usual currency, depending on how many stops he had already made on his journey.

His sermons were usually held at our house, packed to the rafters with local worshippers. He would chain-smoke throughout, and the heavier the sermon, the deeper he would draw on his cigarette as he watched the weight of his words take effect.

He would then carefully place his rolled-up cigarette next to the burning incense, before continuing, '... And if you listen to any kind of music, you will descend into the fires of hell!'

This was too much for a pair of teenagers just discovering the joys of the Beatles and Tom Jones. My brother, Shahid, pushed the mullah's cigarette into the burning lumps of incense, creating a smell from hell.

The mullah continued nodding sage-like as he watched his awful words sink in and reached for his roll-up, but the cigarette had now vanished somewhere in the burning incense.

As the mullah desperately groped in the coals, his anger turned to incandescent rage.

'... And if any of you are unfortunate enough to actually *play* a musical instrument, you are most certainly doomed!'

The congregation visibly trembled.

'And you will be thrown into a burner designed not just for you but for all those other merchants of lewdness and lechery: prostitutes, singers and dancers. You'll feel your brain bubble while the rest of you withers away!'

By now most of the male congregation – musicians, singers and dancers of the local *Hayawi* and *Hacha'a* style – were in tears, pleading for the mullah to forgive them.

On one occasion, the mullah left us to visit the house next door, where the children sat in a circle around him enjoying their sweets and toys. Unfortunately for the mullah, he had given us nothing since his arrival so we decided to take his tobacco pouch as punishment. It was almost full, with about seven pounds of prime scented tobacco that we knew he could never buy locally. We also knew that he would be lost without it, so we hid it in the barn.

'What are we going to do with it?' Shahid wondered.

'Let's mix it with some manure!'

Shahid loved the idea and, within a few seconds, we'd added a delicate mix of manure and powdered incense to his tobacco pouch.

We returned to our neighbour's house and while I kept the mullah busy, my brother put the exotic blend back into his saddlebag.

Shahid and I watched in anticipation as the mullah reached for his tobacco pouch, rolled, then lit his first smoke of the evening. He looked as if he had inhaled neat mustard gas, the way his cheeks went a reddish yellow and his eyes seemed to almost pop out of their sockets. He coughed so violently his turban flew off his head, landing in the middle of the shocked congregation.

My brother solemnly picked it up, handed it back and asked loudly, '*Mawlana*, my lord, how's your tobacco?'

'No good at all; I've been cheated! The oppressors may have sold me bad tobacco, but don't worry, God will punish them and I'll be back to watch them suffer!'

7

Salman was in his forties, a man of honour, but dangerous. He was the proud owner of the finest horse in the region. Everyone wanted to buy it, but Salman loved his horse more than anything, believing only he deserved it.

Salman's wife wanted to sell the horse to bring in some money, but if Salman couldn't have it, nobody would.

One morning, while my father was away, my mother called me urgently: 'I want you to go to Salman's house, get his horse and bring it back here, as quickly as you can!'

According to Salman's wife, he had had enough of her bickering and was now threatening to shoot his pride and joy.

Common sense told me to avoid Salman till the trouble blew over, and soon after I began the walk to Salman's place, I turned back.

I was twelve years old and in tears.

'Mama, I'm scared! What if he shoots me?' I cried, hoping she might change her mind.

'Don't be silly! Salman won't shoot you; he just wants to shoot the horse!'

'But I'll be on it!' I whimpered.

'Listen to me', she said firmly, 'you are the only man here. When Salman sees you riding his horse he won't shoot because he respects our family. Besides, that thoroughbred is his most precious possession. Be brave and good luck!'

By now, Salman's wife was crying too, her children huddled around her, as I set off once again for Salman's.

First I had to pass his dog, a black and white brute, resembling nothing I had ever seen before or since. Whenever we met, he would start with a low growl that became louder as he crawled closer, his chest pressed tight to the ground. When his backside began to rise, that was my cue to sprint for home as fast as my legs could carry me, but there he would be, sprinting behind like a greyhound, slavering saliva left and right.

This time things were different. The dog saw me coming but didn't move. He was clever, this creature. He was leaving me for Salman.

I ran past the dog, jumped over the stream and the spiked fence beyond, before reaching the stable unscathed.

Salman was nowhere to be seen but there, inside the stable, stood the thoroughbred, agitated, whinnying, his tail swishing wildly.

Overwhelmed by his beauty – perfect unity between head, neck, shoulders and legs – I saw gentleness and kindness shining from pleading, dark eyes that caught my gaze for a moment. He was a brown *Kuhail*, full and rounded, with a bright white flash down his face.

Salman had always boasted that this horse would easily pass the ultimate test of speed and stamina: the egg test. According to Salman, if a horse could stand on an egg, three-quarters of which was buried in the sand, without breaking it, he was a genuine thoroughbred.

As the horse began to tire, I stroked his neck whispering words of reassurance. Untying his halter, I felt a raw surge of energy pouring from that huge shoulder directly into mine: it was as if we were one and the same creature, destined to live or die together.

I quickly led him to a small gap in the fence, grabbing a horse blanket on the way. As I threw it across his back, a small group had gathered, watching our every move from beyond the river. It was winter and it was cold.

Making what seemed the perfect leap onto those broad, shining shoulders, I briefly touched the blanket, before landing in a jumbled heap on the other side. How the crowd cheered!

If an Arab falls from his horse, he smiles broadly to show everyone he is alright, then remounts. This time, though, it was hard to smile. Salman was running towards me in his long johns, waving a double-barrelled shotgun.

I remounted, knowing that there was little I could do if he chose to use it. Only Allah could save me now.

'Sayed Maged! Get off that horse!'

No answer.

As Salman came closer, the silence was shattered as he let loose a barrel into the early morning sky.

I froze.

My support melted into the shadows. Now there were just three of them: the horse, Salman's wife and my mother, whose words 'Be brave' still echoed in my ears.

By the time Salman ordered me off his horse for the third time, he was only a few yards away, the shotgun pointed straight at my chest.

For an Arab, the only thing worse than sitting on his horse is to sit on his wife. You risk death on both counts but, by now, Salman was so angry I was convinced he was about to fire the second barrel at me.

'I'm telling you, get off that horse!' Salman shouted, as he clung on desperately to the halter. 'I've told the woman, I am going to kill it and that's final.'

Then I did something extraordinary. My tongue unwound as I stammered something about my father being at home. Although I was lying through my teeth, I was sure that God would look after me in my hour of need, especially after what I'd already been through!

The atmosphere changed immediately. Salman lowered his gun and stepped back, letting go of the halter, before solemnly asking me to give my word that I was telling the truth. 'Are you sure?'

He knew my father had been away for days. What if he thought I was bluffing?

Desperate, I carried on regardless. 'Yes, I swear by Allah! He's at home and wants to see you right away!' I realised then that Salman's respect for my father would see me through.

'In that case, you can keep the damn thing. And if you don't want it, I'll kill it later!'

8

Whenever I look back at my schooldays, instead of feeling proud of my achievements in the classroom or sports field, I somehow feel a sense of opportunities missed.

Now that I think about it, it was no wonder. I was surrounded by three lovable idiots most of the time: Shahid, Ghadi and Deewan.

My brother, Shahid, was a year older than me. He was rarely up to much good; a bit of a dunce really, particularly at maths, but he'd been my first and best buddy for as long as I could remember.

As the dreaded maths exam approached Shahid became more depressed: he'd heard that if he failed, his time in the army could be doubled from two years to four!

Despite all-night revision, private tutorials and valium, the pressure eventually got to him. Shahid couldn't stand it a moment longer and begged me to sit the exam for him and, foolishly, I agreed.

The papers were set by the National Board of Education, using supply teachers as observers, so the risk of my being recognised was minimal as Shahid and I were almost identical.

When the big day came Shahid was hanging round the school gates as I confidently strode into the exam hall, sat down and contemplated my strategy for success. I would read the exam paper, select the five easiest questions, write the answers, then finish before the headmaster appeared, usually after about an hour.

I had barely started question one when I felt a tap on my shoulder and heard a voice whisper quietly in my ear, 'Where's Shahid?'

It was the headmaster.

'What do you mean, Sir? I *am* Shahid.'

'No you're not; you're his brother, Maged. He was here yesterday and I can tell you he looks nothing like you! Put your pen away and come with me.'

Everyone in the exam hall stopped writing to get a better look. A hundred pairs of eyes watched as I followed the headmaster down the corridor.

He opened his study door and, terrified, I walked in first and stood shaking beside his desk.

'This is a very serious matter, Maged, and I should call the police, but you come from a good family so I am going to call your father first. While I do that, go and get Shahid. I almost ran him over by the school gates on the way in!'

Shahid was still there, pacing up and down, smoking furiously. Before we'd had a chance to work out what to do next my eldest brother, Hamoud, arrived and marched us straight to the headmaster's study.

He held us both by our collars as he assured the head that, whatever he chose to do, we would be severely dealt with at home.

Amazingly, the headmaster sent us home unpunished and allowed Shahid to resit the maths exam after the holiday – to everyone's surprise, he passed.

Shahid only had to revise, but I was expected to work in the family bakery all summer without pay.

Ghadi was a maniac and I loved him for it.

We were students together at the textile college in al-Kut and became friends because he was game for anything.

Once, after a physics class about the laws of gravity, he went up to the first-floor balcony and threw himself off to find out how long it took to land.

Ghadi was unusual: it took him well over a year to realise that the portrait of the nation's leader had changed from al-Bakr to Saddam Hussein.

'Who on earth's that guy on the wall?' Ghadi asked, totally unaware of the publicity, posters and razzmatazz that had been rammed down the nation's collective throat continuously for the past twelve months.

It was around that time we were given a particularly detailed assignment on textiles. Most students went to the local *souk* to look in the shops and gather fashion information, but not Ghadi. He chose to stand by the main Basra highway and record every vehicle that passed in the minutest detail: the make, the model, the colour; and then the type: car, trailer or flatbed. What all this transport information had to do with textiles, only Ghadi knew.

He didn't stop there, noting the number of passengers, registration numbers and any unusual markings. No detail was too much for Ghadi.

After dodging countless buses and lorries and logging their details, he returned with yards of information that he proudly presented to his classmates and our bewildered teacher.

'The volume of traffic has a major bearing on the supply routes for the textile industry: the Basra highway needs to be widened!'

The teacher congratulated Ghadi on his painstaking research, and suggested he might like to work at the Transport Ministry, or better yet, become the minister himself.

Like most young pupils in Iraqi schools and colleges, Ghadi and I were recruited to join the ruling Ba'ath Party. Most sixteen-year-olds were organised into party cells, each cell consisting of about fifteen members who, under the supervision of a senior party member, would elect a cell leader. I was chosen because, at six foot two, I was the tallest.

As cell leader I was expected to read the official Ba'ath Party literature and lecture my comrades twice a week on the party line towards Unity, Liberty and Socialism.

One day, when we had a particularly important party meeting, my mother was cooking *dolma* and spring lamb for lunch: this was one meeting I would have to miss. I appointed my friend Ghadi as my deputy, told him to take charge of the meeting, and suggested he take everyone to the market. There they could mingle with the shoppers and ask their views on Liberty and Freedom.

Ghadi loved the idea.

By now all that mattered was my mother's *dolma* and, just as we were setting off – me to lunch and everyone else to the market – the senior Ba'ath Party official marched in.

'What's going on, comrades? Where the hell are you all going?' he asked.

46

'Comrade Maged suggested we move the meeting to the market to find out the public's views on Liberty and Freedom,' Ghadi replied, saluting.

'Sit down, all of you! You can't do that! All questions and answers concerning Freedom and Liberty are written here in this booklet!' screamed the Ba'ath man.

By now, he was brandishing one of Saddam's party leaflets, which made clear how little Liberty and Freedom meant to him.

Then the party official asked what I had in mind by taking my cell to market.

'It is important for the cell to mingle with the working class. If our Ba'ath revolution is to succeed, we need the peasants on our side!' I replied.

'Where did you get that idea, young man?'

'*The Little Red Book*. Mao Zedong, sir!'

The Ba'ath man was livid, telling the rest of the cell to ignore my comments: the Ba'ath Party had no need for idiots like me and Ghadi. We were dismissed on the spot and told to leave the building without further delay, arriving at the table as the houmous and mother's bread were about to be served.

The lamb and *dolma* followed soon after.

Deewan was my first adult friend.

I was eleven: he was nearer forty, an inventor known as 'Newton' and, like most inventors, he had an opinion about everything. This was a quality viewed with suspicion by most people, but it was the very quality I most admired about him and, pretty soon, we were in business together.

Our friendship developed soon after I complained to Deewan

about a toy car he had created from a lump of wood nailed to four cans of Hungarian tomato puree, dragged along on a piece of string. The wheels were so badly aligned that wherever I dragged it, it could only go sideways: as a work of art, it had some merit but as a working toy it was useless.

From this our business partnership was born: from now on, I would take charge of design, while he would be responsible for manufacture and sales.

First, we came up with a revolutionary idea for combs. The new all-wood design was good for blood circulation and guaranteed to slow baldness. We were convinced that our discovery would mark the renaissance of Arab invention, on hold since the thirteenth century. The comb was made of polished oak and solid as rock; in fact, blood circulation would be so improved it would be flowing down our customers' necks.

Our next invention was the BP shower unit. The design was simplicity itself: a large, empty BP oil drum made of tin, painted BP green. Not quite as dark as the Islamic green, but near enough for customers to believe that cleanliness was, indeed, next to Godliness. In fact, little did most of our customers realise just how close to God they actually came.

The business plan was that Deewan should sell the empty oil drum, take the money, then install it complete with hose and sprinkler attached, supported by a couple of poles provided by the client, thick enough to support the drum when filled with ten gallons of water.

The problem was that, instead of using two sturdy poles, as agreed, Deewan would usually skimp and make do with just one, using it to wedge the water-filled drum against the mud-brick wall, while using the second pole to tether his horse outside before selling it on.

Sir Isaac Newton would have had a seizure seeing his laws of gravity treated with such disdain as, usually, the whole contraption would eventually come crashing down: oil drum, timber, wall and all.

Complaints poured in, but Deewan would always blame the customer for supplying bad timber and failing to take seriously enough the skull and crossbones clearly marked on every drum. With Deewan it was a case of 'Shower at your peril ... it may well be your last.'

A few years later, Deewan was sent to prison for life after killing Salman.

Deewan was a follower of a dignitary called Mohan who wanted to buy Salman's horse. Salman was so incensed by Mohan's insistence that he threw his shoe at Mohan's head, whereupon Deewan wasted no time restoring the tribe's honour by shooting Salman dead on the spot.

A messenger was sent to al-Hay to inform the police and, a few hours later, a jeep arrived to arrest Deewan, who refused to surrender until the police had taken tea with him first.

Deewan argued that he was merely protecting the honour of his tribe, and now the police were adding insult to injury by refusing his kind hospitality.

Eventually, the arresting officers agreed to take tea with Deewan: not at his house, but at the house of a relative.

After a final sip of sweet tea, he was led away and later sentenced to life imprisonment.

Sadly, I never saw Deewan again. I remember chasing the police jeep and throwing stones at them because they wouldn't let me say goodbye to him. I also remember Deewan waving back at me and shouting, 'Don't worry, it'll be a doddle. I'll make you a new car!'

Soon after our partnership was born, Deewan lent me eleven dinars (£20 in those days) to apply for a passport, and suggested I repay him from my first wages, whenever that would be. Fearing my father's reaction, he made me promise not to tell anyone about our secret. Unfortunately, I never had a chance to repay his kindness as, soon after his arrest, Deewan died in Abu Ghraib prison.

9

My father's title meant that we children inherited the privileges he enjoyed, passed on by his father and his father's father before him. People would bow, curtsey and kiss our hands – all part of the Shi'ite belief that through this direct link with the Prophet Himself, God's compassion will, one day, prevail over oppression and injustice. (Despite the courtesies shown my family over the years, that happy day still seems some way off.)

There were times when being a Sayed proved to be more of a pain than a privilege. Shahid and I were always on the lookout for girls, but local ones were out of the question. The problem was that locals of both sexes, young and old, expected us sons of a Sayed to behave like gentlemen.

Our teenage desires meant we must try our luck elsewhere: about ten miles from al-Moraibi, at Lake Saeedya.

After putting on our designer *dish-dash*[1] we forced the lock of

---

1. An ankle-length shirt commonly worn with an Arab headscarf called *shimagh*.

our elder brother's sex cabinet for a bit of Brut here, Toledo there and a splash of Lee Van Cleef all over.

How could any girl resist us now?

My dream was to find two lusty females: a pretty one for me, and whatever was left for my brother.

Today, God willing, Lake Saeedya, 'the Place of Plenty' would live up to its name.

Lake Saeedya lay in the centre of what looked like a large flat bowl about two miles square, surrounded by rolling hills, and overlooked to the south by the ancient city walls of Wasit, once the home of the notorious *Wali*[1] of Iraq, al-Hajjaj, scourge of the Sayeds.

Rumour had it that al-Hajjaj would first strip his victims, then drag them over dried straw before dousing them in vinegar. We imagined we could still hear their screams, or was it al-Hajjaj screaming at his Sayed prisoners to keep the noise down?

Shahid and I would challenge each other to see who could pee the furthest along the Wasit city walls: a mild protest against the evil al-Hajjaj and his barbarism.

This time, however, we reached the city ruins and, looking down into the valley, could hardly believe our eyes. There, playing by the lake, were two exquisitely beautiful young ladies.

Shahid and I jostled for the best possible view to savour the moment unobserved: there they were, two dream girls, one rounder than the other, sitting together by the edge of the lake, skirts tucked to the waist, their long legs splashing in clear blue water.

'We'll walk casually towards them and invite them to play hide-and-seek,' Shahid suggested.

---

1. Governor. Iraq was ruled for nearly one hundred years from Damascus by the al-Hajjaj's Umayyad dynasty of the eighth century AD.

We'd thought about a swim, but mixed bathing is forbidden in the Muslim world. A traditional game like hide-and-seek stood a much better chance of success.

The fact that there was nowhere to hide was to our advantage; all we had to do was persuade the girls to play the game underwater.

As we coolly approached our quarry, they stood up and made what looked like encouraging gestures: nervous giggles and a shy turn of the shoulder that seemed to say, 'Come and get us!'

I was ready to run for home but, before I could move, Shahid managed to speak:

'Er, would you, er, like a game of hide-and-seek?'

'We have to go quite soon,' the pretty one replied.

'A quick game ... please!'

Just then, as the girls seemed ready to agree, the one person we hated from al-Moraibi appeared in the distance: the dreaded Fadhil.

Soon he was just a few hundred yards away, heading straight towards us.

There was something strange about Fadhil. He was the same age and went to the same school as me, but he was fixated by my status as a Sayed, endlessly bowing and kissing my hands, something only adults normally did.

It was my hand he always wanted to kiss, never Shahid's.

Seeing him come, I turned to my brother and said, 'What do we do now?' knowing full well that, whatever he might suggest would be to my disadvantage, for Shahid was shrewd, cunning and sixteen, a year older than me.

'Dip your hands in the mud. It's the only way to stop him doing all that kissing stuff! Go on, he's almost here!'

I looked at Fadhil, then the girls, and plunged both my arms deep into the mire.

When I stood up again, Fadhil was standing right next to me as he grabbed my filthy, mud-soaked hand and kissed it passionately, while I shouted at him to leave me alone.

As Fadhil ran back towards the Wasit Walls, one of the girls cried out, 'You must be a Sayed!'

Before I could reply, my brother answered 'Yes, it's true; I *am* a Sayed and this is my friend. Let's go to your house and have him washed!'

While Shahid walked arm in arm with his new-found admirer, the other girl ran off, leaving just the three of us heading for the round one's house.

When we arrived, she showed me the bathroom first, then it was Shahid's turn for a quick wash and brush-up.

While he was away grooming himself, the girl opened a curtain to reveal an ancient Westinghouse refrigerator without a door. A couple of chickens jumped from the middle shelf onto the floor as she yanked open the freezer at the top and brought out a jug of water.

'I'm sorry it's not cold, but the village hasn't got electricity yet!'

She started telling me about her mother who was at the market and due home soon so, when Shahid eventually emerged from the bathroom, I took him to one side and volunteered to act as look-out while he got on with the job.

'I'll keep watch outside and, if anyone comes in, tell them you're here to service the fridge.'

I left the house and waited. Before long, a short, stocky woman approached and headed straight for the door with her shopping bags.

A few moments later, Shahid shot out of the front door, zigzagging left and right, the mother close behind shouting and cursing, beating him with a broom.

'Please, don't hit me! Please! It's true, I'm here to service the fridge! Ouch, ya *gahba*!'[1]

---

1. The Iraqi slang for bitch; *sharmouta* in the rest of the Arab world.

10

It was the sixth anniversary of the 1967 Six-Day War or the 'June Setback', as it was called in the Arab world, when Egypt, Syria, Jordan and Iraq combined to launch their abortive attack on Israel. The intention was to reclaim Arab land on behalf of the homeless driven from Palestine to create the State of Israel in 1948 but, as the world knows well, the June Setback was a humiliating Arab defeat.

In fact it was much more than that: the failure of the Six-Day War was the biggest disaster to affect the Arabs since the Mongol sack of Baghdad in 1258.

In 1947 the United Nations had agreed, in the face of strong Arab opposition, to partition Palestine into two independent states, one Arab and the other Jewish.

The arid parts, Gaza and the West Bank, were for the Palestinians, and the coastline and fertile plain were for the Jewish people to set up their own State of Israel. Jerusalem, capital of the West Bank, was to remain in Arab hands as it had since the Crusades.

However, in just six days of fighting in June 1967 all was lost and more, Israel occupying both Gaza and the West Bank, the Egyptian Sinai Desert as far as the Suez Canal and Syria's Golan Heights. Most serious of all, Jordan had lost Jerusalem: after Mecca and Medina, Islam's third holiest shrine for over fourteen hundred years.

As a result, all Arabs, particularly Iraqis, had to pay for this loss through higher taxes, lower standards of living and the rise of dictatorship, affecting the psyche and neurotic condition of Arab nations and individuals alike in a way that is not yet fully understood.

This is part of the more recent Arab tragedy, never better illustrated than through the lives of two of my Iraqi friends, Leelo and Fairouz.

Leelo was a school-friend from al-Moraibi, gentle and serene, unusually blond and, as one who stood out from the crowd, always bullied. Even the teachers would pick on him. His father was so upset by the bullying he decided to alter Leelo's papers and volunteer him for the army.

'It'll make a man of him,' he insisted.

Everyone complained that Leelo was only fifteen, but his father would have none of it. Leelo was accepted into the military without question.

In October 1973, when we were both sixteen, Leelo was sent to the front line in the Golan Heights, never to return. Nobody even knew how he died, so I convinced anyone I could that Leelo had died bravely defending his position to the last. Lying about how he died, rather than telling the truth about his tragic life, seemed the only way to honour his memory.

We Arabs had become a nation of liars, all in it together to keep up morale, for how else were we to keep going? So spectacular had been our defeat that the worldly well of human kindness had dried up. For the West, the Arab military was now a laughing stock.

I even lied to myself about Leelo's grave and imagined the words on his headstone: 'Leelo, straight to the tomb from his mother's womb.'

Later that same year a crowd of several thousand protesters gathered in al-Kut to demonstrate against Israel's occupation of Jerusalem. The mayor was giving a speech on how the Arab nation might yet recover from the loss when one of the protesters interrupted, grabbing the microphone. To the jubilation of the crowd he vowed that, from this moment on, he would never shave again until he had helped liberate Jerusalem from the Zionists.

The mayor praised this patriotic gesture before another man, a thoughtful type in his forties, calmly took over the microphone to denounce such a protest as meaningless.

His point was simple. 'It is useless making emotional and empty gestures, when first we must look at ourselves.'

Asked by the mayor to explain, the man paused for a moment, his eyes scanning the ground as if searching for something, before looking up:

'From this moment on, I will give up my job as a librarian to become a full-time street cleaner. I would like everyone here to join me cleaning the streets in their spare time for, if we are to liberate the Holy City of Jerusalem, we must clean our own city first!'

A few cheered but it was the one who offered just his face to the cause that drew the loudest applause. The other, offering his whole being, was rejected.

After a year, the first protester, now heavily bearded, pleaded unsuccessfully for the mayor to release him from his vow. Eventually, when the mayor was transferred, he was allowed to shave and joined the local Ba'ath Party.

The librarian, however, kept his word and swept the streets of al-Kut each day without complaint or pay. Wherever the city was cleanest, there you would find the librarian pushing his broom.

Finally, his family disowned him, but he carried on sweeping for a few more years, his spirit undimmed, his body now little more than skin and bone.

To the locals of al-Kut, he became known as Fairouz, after the celebrated Lebanese *chanteuse* whose song 'Flower of Cities' was to become the Arab anthem of hope that Jerusalem would, one day, be free.

I remember the last time I met Fairouz.

'Why are you still cleaning the streets?' I asked.

He leant on his broom with a resigned, tired smile, his eyes barely open.

'Jerusalem still isn't free and the streets of al-Kut are no cleaner than when I started!'

11

National service in Iraq is compulsory for anyone over eighteen and, as a full-time student, I did my best to delay the draft for as long as I could but, after a three-year course in textiles, the army finally caught up with me.

I was now nineteen and, after three months basic training, I was one of twelve conscripts assigned to a unit specialising in the manufacture of military decorations such as stars, eagles and swords. Some of the most important medals of all – for valour and bravery – we kept for ourselves, just in case. We also made enormous trophies for the army football and basketball leagues, but it was the gold medallions for soldiers' girlfriends that paid for our nights out in Baghdad.

After a few months settling into army life we dug a hole under the wire fence and took it in turns to sneak out into the city. The only impediment was the sergeant. A kindly man, he was dedicated to his job and to his lunch, which he would bring with him in a traditional Iraqi *safer-tas* – with rice in the largest bowl , stewed meat and sauce in the next, and so on, with the smallest bowl at the top containing a lamb kebab or some chicken. Somewhere in the middle there might be a variety of tasty condiments: sauces, such as yoghurt and dried raspberries to go with the lamb or homemade sweet and sour relish for the chicken.

The sergeant's meal always included a salad that he prepared himself before the lunch break and, as the route to a man's heart is through his stomach, so our route to Baghdad was paved with salad. We convinced the sergeant that from now on we, his loyal men, would prepare his lunch.

Determined to get away one afternoon, I insisted on preparing him a special salad, a mixture of cucumber, tomato, onion and olives, drenched in garlic sauce and vinegar. All this, sitting on top of his stewed lamb and fried rice, was sure to send him to sleep and, after his last mouthful of goat's cheese saturated in the heaviest ghee, there was a triumphant burp, then silence. He was out like a light. I made my escape under the wire fence and soon I was strolling along the river-bank, beret in hand. In twenty minutes I would be at the bus stop in Caradet-Mariam, ready for my big day out, and a film about the life and times of Charlie Chaplin which was to open later that evening at the Babel Cinema – an event sure to attract the best looking girls in Baghdad. This would be the perfect opportunity to show off my new Alain Delon hairstyle – fashioned after the famous French film star of the time, who attracted girls by casually running his fingers through his hair while looking longingly in their direction.

I was dreaming of beautiful girls and paradise when suddenly, out of nowhere, a military police foot patrol appeared from behind the palm trees demanding to see my pass.

Persuasion was hopeless and, before I knew what was happening, I was under arrest. This would mean a 'zero' haircut for being absent without leave and at least two months before I could run my fingers through my gelled hair again. By now, Brylcreem was a hot commodity in Baghdad and I had boxes of it courtesy of my brother's latest girlfriend, whose father happened to be the sole importer of the stuff to Iraq.

The guards radioed for a car to escort me back to my unit. My hopes were raised when Russia's worst attempt yet to enter the competitive car market arrived – a Zil – and promptly broke down.

While we waited, one of the guards tried to impress me with his knowledge of the more obscure sights of Baghdad.

'Do you know who lived in that villa over there?' he asked, pointing somewhere in the distance.

I shook my head.

'Agatha Christie. She got married there,' the guard nodded arrogantly.

On the way back to barracks I remembered a short preview I had read about an Agatha Christie movie, *Murder on the Orient Express*, a suspense story with false trails, twists and turns so complex that, in this hour of need, it was to Agatha I turned, not Allah. Her talent for intrigue might yet save me from the dreaded zero haircut.

That afternoon I stood before my commanding officer.

'Conscript 342616, sir!' I shouted, saluting.

As I stamped my boots together, the steel doors slammed shut behind me. Bright sunlight shone into my eyes like a searchlight from above, and dust spun up from the hard, concrete floor to the window. The CO sat dutifully behind his desk reading the charge sheet, dust settling on his short, neat haircut.

'As you were, soldier!' He looked up from my file, then down again.

Silence.

I prayed that my attempt to make an impressive entrance hadn't backfired. He hadn't kept me standing to attention too long: a promising sign as, sometimes, you could be kept standing to attention for an eternity before even a word was spoken.

'Explain your cowardly behaviour ... and it had better be good!'

'Me, sir?'

I must have looked pathetic, glancing round the room in the forlorn hope that he might be addressing someone else, hiding in a cupboard, perhaps.

The officer tore off his glasses and looked me straight in the eye.

'So, why did you leave without permission?'

'I had to do it, sir!' I replied passionately.

'You had to do it ... Why?' he asked intrigued.

'I discovered that Agatha Christie once lived in Caradet-Mariam. Curiosity got the better of me. I just had to go there.'

'Who on earth is Agatha Christie?'

'Sir, Agatha Christie is a great woman who predicts the future in her books. These books are then made into films and, so far, all her predictions have come true and, apparently, she was here in Iraq to predict our future and make a film about it.'

The officer appeared deep in thought, as he invited me to take a seat.

'Tell me more, son.'

I started to spin a tale of political intrigue around the work of not just Agatha Christie but William Shakespeare, Shylock and his trickery and Henry V, with a touch of Sir Anthony Eden and the Suez Crisis thrown in for good measure. Any story that showed up the Jews, or the West, in a negative light was always well received: to combine the two was considered the finest delicacy.

The officer seemed fascinated by my breakthrough in military intelligence. Slowly he stood up and, with a nod of admiration, shook my hand and earnestly thanked me for introducing him to the work of Agatha Christie.

'And furthermore, I totally exonerate you of all charges and if there is anything I can do for you in the future, please let me know.'

I saluted again, as more dust spun its way up towards the bright, sunlit window.

I turned for the door.

'One more thing, son. Next time you want to leave the barracks, kindly use the front gate!'

After that, I was sharing a flat in the centre of Baghdad with my brother, Saeed, a law student with an afternoon job at the State Cement Establishment. It was a privileged position, as the cement industry was enjoying a building boom that had continued since the nationalisation of the oil industry in 1972. My brother's office was situated right outside al-Rasheed barracks; the perfect opportunity for me to combine my military duties with some cement sales. Luckily, I had been chosen by my unit to arrange delivery of all the medals and decorations for the various regimental presentation ceremonies. This meant I could associate with the officer class, who were always looking for favours (a silver-plated medallion for the wife and a gold one for the girlfriend). They would often invite me into the Officers' Club or, at least, offer me a cigar after the initial business was over. That was the cue to make my pitch.

'If you need cement, I'm your man!'

It never failed and, within minutes, we would be on our way to my brother's office, siren blaring, the driver instructed to proceed at full speed ahead, as my new partner and I sat in the back, each smoking a Montecristo cigar, discussing how to split the profits. In fact, the only profit that concerned me was the amount of leave I might get.

By the time the order was signed and we had finished our State Cement coffee, the officer would be convinced that the deal was as solid as my cement and any leave papers would be waiting at the sergeant's office within the hour.

My reputation as the cement kid of Baghdad spread like wildfire.

Once, I turned up at my brother's office accompanied by a particularly greedy officer who told me that he needed twenty bags to renovate his bathroom. But as soon as he sat down with my brother, he raised his order from twenty bags to two hundred.

Saeed whisked me to one side. 'What are you trying to do to me? I thought you said he was building a bathroom, not a runway!'

I must have taken orders for half of Iraq's annual cement production but I only received a few bags, which I sold to my kindly sergeant at cost, in return for two weeks' leave.

12

By 1979 I was twenty-two and had lived through the final year of the Iraqi monarchy, as well as the four military coups that followed. I'd seen how each change of government had brought its own brand of fear and suspicion affecting almost every family in Iraq. Arrest, imprisonment, torture, even execution were commonplace.

After ten years of political and economic stability under the leadership of General al-Bakr, Iraqis were ready to settle their differences and build a great new nation that would be the envy of the world. By nationalising the oil industry, Iraq's greatest resource, petrodollars were now pouring into the nation's coffers and, as a result, some salaries were up by as much as fifty per cent. A programme to improve education, health and the country's infrastructure was now bearing fruit and Iraq seemed to be almost overflowing with milk and honey. In the opinion of many enjoying this boom, it was the deputy president, Saddam Hussein, who had delivered the goods.

Eleven years earlier, al-Bakr had masterminded the coup that saw President Arif off on a plane to Algiers. He was the first Iraqi head of state to leave office alive. The previous three – King Feisal II and Presidents Kassem and Arif Senior – hadn't been so lucky.

For a few days leading up to the anniversary of this 'White Revolution', the people of Iraq were subjected to a relentless torrent of Ba'athist propaganda via the newspapers, radio and television promising, of all things, free elections and federation with Syria.

That was the last Iraqis were to hear about either.

These exciting announcements were accompanied by even more extraordinary pictures, hourly television updates featuring the daily activities of the country's Deputy President, Saddam Hussein. In a single day we would see Saddam waking farm workers at six in the morning wearing his overalls and wellington boots, then leading them out of their dormitories to the fields; next he'd be seen in a white coat and hard hat at some building project the other end of the country; then kissing Kurdish babies and taking tea in a residential estate wearing a Kurdish *shirwal*;[1] finally, visiting hospitals and touching the patients, as if healing the sick, in his Pierre Cardin suit holding a large unlit Cohiba cigar.

This was the man now credited by the media for these past ten years of peace and prosperity, as if al-Bakr had never existed. This was the man who saw himself as the new Saladin, the future liberator of Jerusalem who would restore honour to the Arab nation.

Iraq's new dawn had finally arrived.

It was 16 July, the eve of the eleventh anniversary of the coup that had brought al-Bakr and Saddam to power.

Everybody was out on the streets by early evening to dance,

1. All-in-one shirt and trousers worn by Kurds, traditionally topped with a turban.

listen to the bands and join in the celebrations. I sat with a couple of friends in a Baghdad café sipping coffee. One was Fadhil, the hand-kisser from al-Moraibi, who'd recently signed up for a further five years in the army, the other, a friend of his from Military Intelligence.

The Ba'ath Party commercial played on the radio in the background:

> Our path to excellence is lonely and long;
> So too are our hopes,
> But every blessing takes a long time.
> The years will pass
> And the Ba'ath shall remain
> For, beyond time, there is a beautiful dream:
> The seeds of life are within us
> And the unique Ba'ath shall remain unique.

It was the same party political broadcast that had been aired every day, three times a day, for the past ten years. Trilling flutes, oboes, violins and a seafaring concertina introduced the sexiest female voice in Iraq:

'This is the *Voice of the People*, Baghdad!'

A drum roll followed by a cymbal crash, then the Iraqi equivalent of Barry White slowly reciting the Ba'ath monologue in a deep, husky bass before announcing:

'Iraq, on the march to Jerusalem and Arab unity!'

We were admiring the victory arches and decorations that now covered every corner of Baghdad when, suddenly, we heard a muffled explosion. The next thing I knew, my friends were leaping from their seats and running in the direction of the blast. I quickly followed, catching up as they reached an alleyway at the back of a cinema. All I could see was a mass of upturned refuse bins and, beyond, a cloud of thick dark smoke.

We were the first on the scene as, through the haze, a man staggered towards us, his face covered in blood. I could see the fear in his eyes as he cried out for help in Kurdish.

Fadhil screamed out, 'He's a Kurd. Let's get him!'

In a single move, Fadhil punched him in the face and threw him to the ground in a perfect arc, his head hitting the concrete pavement with a sickening crack. Fadhil and his friend then started kicking the man in the face and body as if this was some sort of ritual they'd performed many times before.

They then lifted the poor wretch to his feet, one holding him against the wall, while the other worked on his jaw with merciless lefts and rights.

I pushed Fadhil away and tried to lift the man to his feet, but his friend pushed me away.

'This is none of your business!'

While the three of us argued, the Kurd tried to make a run for it, but now we were joined by another group out for entertainment.

'That's him!' someone shouted, and he was back on the ground receiving another beating.

There was little I could do.

Suddenly, a black Pontiac screeched to a halt near us.

Three security men got out to arrest the poor Kurd.

When I got back to my apartment I turned on the radio. The Ba'ath Party commercial was playing.

The next day Saddam Hussein took over as president of Iraq.

13

It was time to leave Iraq by any means possible.

Arrested for having long hair, I was about to be sent to Harthia Military Interrogation Centre, when a suitable bribe secured my release.

The family bakery had closed down, so money was a problem, and a passport seemed out of the question so for a few weeks I stood outside Baghdad University selling Pepsi. I'd soon saved more than $500.

Unbeknown to my family, I was planning to escape through Turkey.

Arab villagers from the south were encouraged by Saddam to resettle up north in the Kurdish region, while the Kurds were forcibly removed to resettle in the south. Some of my father's friends from al-Moraibi had moved to the area known as the Border Triangle, where Iraq, Turkey and Syria meet, so I caught a bus north to join them.

They'd made the most of their new surroundings, with

telephones, refrigerators, TVs and machine guns, all provided free by the government. I was an honoured guest and they made a great fuss of me, inviting me to coffee meetings, days out and dinner every night. No one suspected the real purpose of my visit. In fact, the local party officials probably suspected I was a spy sent by Baghdad. I did little to allay their suspicions.

I invited the Ba'ath Party chief and his cronies to dine with me and my newfound friends. Our meal of roast lamb and Jack Daniels worked wonders: by the end of the evening not only had my principal guest, the Ba'ath Party chief, paid the bill, but he had fully briefed me on the local security and border controls.

I stayed in a local hotel overnight and, the following morning, the Ba'ath Party chief drove me back to the village in his Land Cruiser.

Just in case my planned escape was to fail, I'd befriended a retired Egyptian general staying in the same hotel, who was touring the region privately by car and meeting his ambassador in Ankara a few days later. I managed to convince the general that I, too, was Egyptian and had lost my passport: could he help? We agreed that, if I managed to clear immigration, he would wait for me just inside the Turkish border, drive me to Ankara, and sort out a new passport with the ambassador. Then we could tour Europe together before returning 'home' to Egypt. It was a trip he made every year. He would visit friends and relatives in Jordan, Iraq and Turkey, before driving on to Europe.

I was convinced, however, that I'd be able to make my escape without the help of the Egyptian general. My plan required a local man, a devil-worshipper called Yazid, to take me to the Turkish border, from where his cousin would drive me on to the nearest Turkish village, where I would take a coach to Diyarbakir, and safety.

We set off at dusk. The air was thick with the scent of almonds as our battered Land Rover bounced over boulders and rocks till, all of a sudden, we stopped. The headlights from a second vehicle flashed; the agreed signal for the devil-worshipper's cousin to reveal himself before taking me on that last lap across the border. We drove another few yards before finally stopping. I grabbed my bag and ran towards the waiting vehicle but, instead of the devil-worshipper's cousin, it was the Ba'ath Party chief. My heart was pumping. Was it a trap, or was he planning to escape, like me?

'Thank God, it's you!' the Ba'ath Party chief shouted, sounding relieved as he beckoned me to join him; 'I never thought you'd make it! Our man's on his way in from Syria!'

What was this about Syria? I thought we were going to Turkey!

Something was definitely wrong.

'What took you so long?' he asked, scanning the hills through his binoculars.

I had to think fast. 'I came as quickly as I could. I would have come earlier, if I'd known it was you!'

'*Al-hamdulilla!* There he is!'

I looked towards the border and, from somewhere, I could hear the sound of stamping, someone gasping for air, but could see nothing. It was like waiting for a ghost when, suddenly, a man appeared rolling down a steep bank towards us. Staggering the last few steps, he collapsed into my arms sobbing.

The Ba'ath Party chief then introduced me to the man whose near-lifeless body we carried to the back of the Land Cruiser. I busied myself with our new passenger, wiping away the blood and sweat and comforting him, while praising his courage. The chief seemed impressed, and clearly relieved by my performance. Luckily he hadn't noticed I'd pissed myself. It'd been that kind of day.

I discovered, as we drove to the Iraqi border post, that the injured man was a senior member of Iraq's secret service, a close relative of Saddam himself from Tikrit, captured weeks earlier on a spying mission to Syria. Here I was, cradling the head of one of Saddam's spymasters.

Amazingly, everyone – my devil-worshipping driver, his cousin, the Egyptian general and most of the village – knew of my escape plan. Everyone except the Iraqi border police.

Early the next day, I packed my bags and caught the bus back to Baghdad. Next time I'd try the legal route. All I needed was a passport.

14

The inconspicuous flat I shared with my brother and a couple of friends in the centre of Baghdad was more like a Soviet outpost in the centre of Moscow. A Russian Embassy car was always parked outside. A Russian Embassy car was always parked outside, driven by a Palestinian who lived on the top floor and who was oblivious to the fact that the electrician and the carpenter sharing the ground floor were both having affairs with his Egyptian wife.

Inside my flat a wooden cabinet, full to the brim with Communist literature, occupied the hall, while a huge poster of Lenin in Red Square covered the toilet wall.

My flatmates, Shakir and Rami, both devoted Communists, were constantly being arrested, tortured then released by Saddam's secret police. This was a well-recognised method of converting Communists into Ba'athists. Shakir would usually sweet-talk his way out of a good hiding and, after his release, would find solace in Tolstoy's *War and Peace*. Rami, a Kurd, was not so lucky. He usually got the wire treatment on his back for starters; then they would strip him naked before making him sit on a broken bottle. He was warned that if he ever visited any hospital for treatment or told anyone about it, even his own mother, he would never see the light of day again; nor would his family.

A few days after my return from my attempted escape, Rami was arrested and so badly tortured he confessed to his interrogators that I, the Palestinian and his Egyptian wife and the carpenter all had Communist tendencies. There was no time to waste.

My only chance of leaving Iraq would be to get a student visa. I needed my army release papers, then security clearance from the police, and finally an English translation of my textile certificate. Luckily, I had the first two.

My textile diploma read simply: 'This certificate is *invalid* for any purpose other than to determine the length of national service and job appointment.'

My brother Saeed was close to one of the receptionists at the British Embassy who organised the required English translation and so, a few days later, I returned to the embassy to collect my textile diploma translated into English.

There was, however, one important change. The translation now read: 'This certificate is *valid* for any purpose other than to determine the length of national service and job appointment.' The only problem was that the British Embassy had attached my original certificate in Arabic above their revised English translation. Anyone comparing the two would discover the deception, now bound together forever with red, white and blue ribbon, sealed in red wax with the stamp of Her Majesty's Consular Section.

I watched nervously as the Director-General of Western European Scholarships examined both documents trying to work out how the Arabic top copy could be 'invalid', while the English copy beneath was 'valid'. He read and reread each sheet slowly and deliberately, turning the top page back and forth, looking up at me.

It was time to bring on Saeed, who had come with me just in case: if anyone could confuse the Director-General, it was Saeed.

'What am I supposed to do with this?' asked the Director, waving the papers in my face.

'Just sign there, sir', replied Saeed, pointing at the dotted line.

'But there's a contradiction between the two: the Arabic original says ...'

Saeed interrupted, assuring the DG that the Arabic was not the original: the English original was underneath, and the word 'valid' was plain for all to see. The Arabic copy was written second, and that's why it was on top: nothing more than just a poor local translation of the English original.

Simple!

The DG signed the exit visa on the spot.

All I needed now was a passport and money for my air fare to London. (All the money I had saved selling Pepsi had been spent on a deposit for a course in England.)

To avoid any bureaucratic delay in Baghdad, I decided to apply for my passport in al-Kut, where I had a friend who was not only an anti-Ba'ath Party diehard, but also a bit of an oddball.

He changed my name, my profession, my height and the colour of my eyes, but it seemed a small price to pay for an Iraqi passport.

My surname he changed from Khedhir to Kadar; my eyes he 'honeyfied' from green to brown: this, and more, so that he could confuse his Ba'athist superiors.

Now I had a passport, I had to perform the hardest task of all:

to convince my parents that it was right that I should leave Iraq for England.

There is an Arab saying that, 'If words are silver, then silence is gold.'

Having never spoken to my parents about my departure plans before, their response was one of sadness and support, but not surprise.

My father stared at the carpet, as if in prayer, before he looked up very slowly, inviting me to sit beside him. Then he put his arm around me.

'If God wills that you should go to England now, then so be it: I have no wish to be held responsible before God, or your mother!

'Go with my blessing and remember your family, your home, the village, the palm groves and the lemon tree but, most of all, remember God's words: "Nothing shall befall us but what God has written for us."'[1]

Five friends joined me that last night in Iraq. It was almost midnight when we reached the lapping waters of the Tigris north of Baghdad. On the river-bank we made beds of palm leaves, shook dates from the trees for the last time, and ate and sang, vowing to meet again under those same trees in happier times, when we would sing and dance the *Chobi*, the traditional dance of Baghdad.

Next morning at the airport, as family and friends hugged each other, laughed and cried together, we said our farewells Iraqi-style:

'*Ma'a salaama*, hello!'

Little did I know that it would be three wars and twenty more years before I saw my family again.

---

1. From the Qur'an: belief in predestination expressed in the popular expression, 'It's all there written on your forehead.'

15

On a wet, windy evening in October 1979, in a state of nervous excitement, this twenty-two-year-old Iraqi stepped off the plane at London Heathrow with his one and only suitcase.

The first thing I noticed was how many airport personnel wore turbans, checking passports or sweeping the customs hall.

'Leave to remain for six months,' the immigration officer announced confidently, stamping my passport.

I was familiar with the words 'leave' and 'remain', but never before in this order so, rather than leave, I remained at his desk.

'How is it possible to leave and remain at the same time?' I asked, mystified.

The officer was in no mood to offer more than the most basic English lesson:

'I've given you leave to remain for the next six months, sir. Now piss off before I change my mind!'

Of all the places I'd contacted, Liverpool had been the only one to respond, offering me a place to study at Kirkby College of

Further Education. So that's where I headed.

In the name of God, the Compassionate, the Merciful ...

Dear Family,

Arrived safely in London greeted by English wind and rain. I have 'leave to remain' for the next six months, so will be working hard to pass my exams to get an extension!

England is full of foreigners. London airport was full of Indians and Liverpool has a large Yemeni community, fewer Iraqis, but all sorts of Muslims and Arabs.

Life in Liverpool is different from al-Moraibi. I saw snow for the first time. Liverpool was as white as my father's soul! Another thing that's different are their tomatoes. They look beautiful, as if they've been drawn by hand, but they don't taste like ours. In fact, they don't taste of anything.

People go to the pub to talk and drink alcohol the way we go to the diwan *to talk and drink coffee. Here, they put milk with their coffee and some don't even add sugar!*

Liverpool people are cheerful, but seem to be slightly mad. My cab driver from the station asked me on the way to Hazim's house where I was from. When I said Baghdad, he immediately remembered Ali Baba and the Forty Thieves, assuring me that I had come to the right place. 'We're all thieves round here!' he said.

It gets cold at night, but I'm coping. I say my prayers and think of you all the time. When I come back, I will bring you some fish and chips. It's indescribable!

I will never forget you, the house, the wooden bridge, the palm groves or the lemon tree. You will always be part of me and I pray for the day when we are together again in al-Moraibi ...

I didn't mention in my letter that Hazim, my friend from Baghdad, was involved in a love triangle with the two other residents, a Welsh girl and the Syrian landlord.

Hazim loved them both and asked me to mediate if I wanted a bed so, after many cups of sweet tea in the kitchen, we agreed that his girlfriend would stay downstairs in Hazim's room rent-free, in return for staying silent about their relationship.

I could stay on the sofa as her non-paying guest on the same condition. Hazim would then move in with his male friend upstairs.

As I filled the empty cupboards and drawers with my clothes, photos and cassettes, I looked out at the walls and white gates of Liverpool Cricket Club.

I lay awake that night thinking about how far I'd travelled from al-Moraibi, my family, the house, the village, the palm groves, the lemon tree and my father's assurance that God would always be with me.

16

A few days later, on a cold, wet Saturday in Liverpool city centre, I found myself wandering around the lingerie section of C&A, where I imagined I might buy something suitably exotic to tempt my landlady, whose only uttering of a sexual nature so far had been to inform me she was 'built like a pit pony', whatever that meant. And there, walking down the aisle towards me, was the most beautiful girl I'd ever seen, blonde and blue-eyed, the perfect English rose.

Our eyes met. She smiled, and I smiled back, then walked upstairs to the menswear department. There she was again, this time with another girl eyeing me up. I knew, if I played my cards right, this could be my lucky day. Sure enough, a week later, I was with Carole and her family for Sunday lunch.

She came to meet me in the city centre accompanied by her father, Tommy, looking every inch the English gentleman in his suit and tie.

'What daily newspaper do you read?' he enquired, shaking me

firmly by the hand.

Was this an English test to see if I was fit to associate with his daughter?

'The *Observer*,' I replied, nervously, unaware that this favourite platform of Pan-Arabists throughout the world is only published on Sundays.

'That's very good. You'll learn good English from the *Observer*, but what do you say when the shopkeeper gives you your paper?'

'I pay him, take it and say, "Thank you."'

'I'm afraid that's not good enough.'

My heart sank.

'In Liverpool we don't just say "Thank you," we say "Thank you, *wanker*!"'

All the way through the Mersey Tunnel and on to Wallasey I was wracking my brains for a translation: the Arab equivalent of *Sayed*, or *Effendi* perhaps?

Arriving at the Hardings' maisonette for lunch, a reception party awaited: there must have been about twenty of them. It was like being back in the family *diwan* in Iraq except, this time, the room was packed with women.

I was introduced to Miriam, Carole's mother, first. She was a fragile, sweet woman, the classic matriarchal figure, wearing a floral pinny over a dress that had clearly seen better days.

'You know, Maj,' she whispered, nodding in the direction of her husband and first cousin, Tommy Harding, 'he's the cause of all my grey hair!'

'See them?' Tommy called back at us, pointing towards Carole and the rest of the girls. 'Just because I slept with their mother, they all think I'm their dad! Ask Nellie Wetlegs what she was doing at two o'clock this morning! Go on, ask her!'

'Terrible, isn't he? Take no notice of him, Maj, he's just showing off.'

Miriam took Tommy's insults in her stride, but women in Iraq might have reacted differently. I remember one who divorced her husband on the spot when he unwisely used a pair of his wife's knickers to pick up a red-hot teapot. His mistake was to do it in front of a visitor. Luckily she loved her ex-husband enough to introduce him to one of her relatives, who soon became his new wife.

Miriam then introduced me to her children one by one.

First, Carole's sister, Jackie:

'You know, Maj, I'm that depressed, I think I'm going to throw myself under a man!'

After Jackie I met Brenda, Carole's eldest sister. She told me all about her husband, Billy, who was 'down the pub', how much she loved him and all about the lunch she had prepared for him earlier that morning, which would be in the oven waiting for him when he got home from playing pool.

Soon it was the grandchildren's turn to introduce themselves.

'Why don't they use cats' arses on the motorway, instead of cats' eyes?' asked little Vicky.

'I have no idea!' I replied.

'Because they'd need twice as many, silly!' she said laughing, then skipped back to her grandfather's lap.

This was a mad house yet, beyond the lunacy, here was a loving and warm-hearted family who all treated me as one of their own.

'We're having Welsh lamb for lunch, the finest meat in England!' Tommy declared loudly, before turning his gaze to me. 'I've cooked it ever so slowly on number five. Welsh lamb grazes by the sea, see? No need to add salt; they're full of it already!

'Just cover him up with a bit of foil to let the flavour flow and, remember, put a dish of water in the oven. It stops the meat shrinking and keeps it moist, and another thing: don't forget to baste the meat from time to time.

'Of course, the secret's putting the right herbs and spices over the lamb first, but that's *my* secret!' Tommy confided, tapping his nose, 'Know what I mean?'

There was no stopping him now.

'Only the best for me, Maj! Take these shoes, I always get the best: got to look after your feet! And these specs; they're the Rolls Royce model: got to look after your eyes!'

By now, the rest of the girls had gathered round: Tommy's cue to announce the next act.

'Maj, if you like, go into the kitchen and do anything you want; then ask me three times, "What am I doing?" and I bet I can tell you!'

Everyone was pleading with me to go into the kitchen, so I agreed.

Carole and I glanced at each other helplessly as I left the room, stepped into a kitchen hotter than a Turkish bath with boiling pots and rattling lids sounding like the drum roll before my execution.

'What am I doing?' Silence. My mouth was beginning to feel dry.

'What am I doing?' Silence, and quiet laughter, as my lips started sticking to each other.

'What am I doing?' I was ready for the worst.

'Fuck all, and you're making a right twat of yourself! Get back in here, you daft Iraqi bugger!'

I returned to cheers and applause, but the show wasn't over yet.

The girls surrounded me on all sides, offering cigarettes, asking questions and comparing heights with each other, all at the same time.

'Do you like Michael Jackson?'

'Do you have the Beatles in Iraq?'

'Do you have hairdryers?'

I smiled, nodded and tried to reply, anxiously looking for Carole, but she was nowhere to be seen. Just as one of the girls was asking me if I believed in God, a hush came over the room: there was Carole with the first pair of plates piled high with roast lamb, vegetables, gravy and Tommy's mint sauce.

I was led, like a lamb to the slaughter, to the head of the table next to Tommy while the rest of the family stood behind their chairs watching us in silence.

I sat down, then they followed, watching me closely, as if waiting for something.

What should I do? Say grace, or eat?

I should have said grace.

I pulled the plate towards me, smiled at my hosts, then plunged my knife and fork deep into the succulent pink meat. Unfortunately, half the plate was balanced over the edge of the table and, as I began to cut into that first slice, the plate and its entire contents tipped warmly into my lap.

Everyone laughed and talked at once, offering their untouched plates, while I did my best to smile.

I chose Carole's.

17

Every day I'd catch the 82C bus from Sefton Park to the Pierhead, buy a red carnation from the flower stall, then catch the Mersey ferry to Wallasey to see Carole and the Harding family.

One afternoon I arrived at the Pierhead as the ferry was slowly pulling away. Rather than face waiting another forty minutes, I took a running jump, grabbed the rail, and hauled myself over before dropping on deck.

Some passengers looked up momentarily from their fish and chips to watch me crawl along the deck, Carole's carnation clenched between my teeth.

It became something of a ritual for Carole to press the red carnation I brought each day carefully inside her Bible. Tommy would greet me at the door with, 'Where's *my* fucking flower, then?'

Carole and I would pick strawberries in Southport, eat oysters in Blackpool and buy fish and chips in Colwyn Bay. We were all gathered in the front room one afternoon for tea and scones, when

Tommy suddenly took off his glasses and pointed them at Carole, 'How long's this going to go on? Do you think he's going to marry you? Of course not: he's using you! Either leave him, or you can leave the house ... now!'

I froze as Carole rose from her armchair.

'Why are you always causing trouble, Dad? I'm eighteen years old and it's none of your business! Look what he's trying to do to me, Mum!'

As Carole sobbed, shoulders trembling, Miriam put the teapot back on the table and walked over to Carole, arms outstretched.

'Don't worry, darling. Maji loves you and that's all that matters!'

Miriam looked at Tommy, then at me, with a look of tired resignation.

'Take no notice of that fat old bastard, Maj. He's trouble. Carole loves you and that's good enough for me. You'll always be welcome in my house!'

I turned towards Tommy. 'What makes you think I'm using Carole?'

Tommy looked up from his paper, 'Are you going to marry her then?'

I couldn't answer. In the three months I'd known Carole I'd never spoken to her about marriage, so I suggested we go to the park over the road, the perfect place for me to propose. I got up from my chair and followed Carole from the room. Carefully, I opened the front door, which we closed behind us with a quiet click. Alone outside at last, we hugged for a brief moment before turning towards Guinea Gap Park.

Tears flowed as we hugged and kissed and declared our love for each other.

'Carole, will you marry me?'

She looked away for a moment, then took a step back still holding my hand firmly.

'Maged, you've no idea what you're letting yourself in for. I love you more than anything in the world, but my dad's a bad man. He hates foreigners and he'll never rest until he's split us up for good, even if we *do* get married.

'We're a poor family. When we were kids Dad, would send us carol singing, sometimes as early as August or September, and if we didn't come back with a pound each he'd leather us with his belt.

'I'm not religious because I've never been christened, so when I started school I'd pretend I was one religion or the other, whichever suited. Catholics beat me up for being a Prod and the Prods beat me up for being a Catholic, so now I just say nothing!

'We'd always get to school late. I remember the teachers used to give us a clock made of paper and ask us to point the arms to the time we went to bed. Most pupils would set the clock to seven or eight. I used to set it on one or two in the morning and the teachers picked on us for telling lies. No one believed us!

'We've had to put up with that all our lives.'

Trying to hold back her tears, Carole bravely carried on, 'I have to put up with him, but *you* don't have to, Maged. You should go to London without me.'

18

We were still on the bench hugging each other, the Mersey swirling beneath us and the Liver Building clock striking five when, suddenly, I had a brainwave.

'Let's go to America and get married! Tommy will never find us there!'

Carole's face lit up. 'I could get our Alan to send you an invitation to get you a visa. I won't have any problem getting one!'

Alan was Carole's brother, a carpenter in Virginia.

'And Alan could help us get work! I'll find a job, work and study at the same time and, once we've got our own place, we could get married!'

Carole agreed immediately.

We phoned Alan with our plan and, a few days later, his letter arrived inviting me to work in his carpentry business. As his sister and my future wife, Carole was invited to come too.

With hopes as high as the fourth of July, Carole and I took a suitcase, our passports and the fast train to London to apply for a future together in America, but joy soon turned to despair when I was granted a visa, but not Carole! Without either a job or a bank account, her application was turned down. We returned to Liverpool broken-hearted and wondering what surprises Tommy might still have in store.

It didn't take long to find out.

A couple of days later, my bank manager phoned to ask if I could pop in to see him urgently. When I arrived he apologised for the inconvenience, thanked me for being so prompt, then handed me a letter.

It was from Tommy, claiming that I planned to rob his bank before escaping back to Iraq.

'Me? Rob Barclays? You must be joking!'

He believed me, but Tommy was clearly determined to keep Carole and me apart. He'd also sent letters to my college, Kirkby College of Further Education, and to the Home Office, telling them that I was an illegal immigrant with a forged passport.

Carole and I were both banned from the house and Tommy's vendetta meant that I was finding it hard to eat or sleep, and was now beginning to doubt my sanity. It was as if Saddam himself was after me.

My patience finally snapped a few days later when, while waiting to meet Carole in a pub, a large wrestler-type walked in, winked, and put his arm round me.

Was this a friend of Hazim or our gay landlord?

'Tommy paid me to sort you out. Gave me twenty quid,' he confided, smiling. 'Don't worry: I took the money but I'm not going to do you. You don't look half as nasty as he says you are! Fancy a pint?'

The following week I was sent to the Liverpool teaching hospital with pneumonia.

Carole came to visit and brought the whole family, including Tommy, who charged up and down the corridors accusing everyone of not doing enough to help me.

Carole held my hand and sobbed, while Jackie told her I had meningitis, and Miriam fed me grapes and tried to calm everyone down.

Tommy returned, sat on my bed, asked the size of my shoes and then explained why:

'I just had a word with Doctor. He thinks you might pull through, but the next few hours are critical!'

Convinced I was close to death, I took the lift to the ground floor, walked through the main doors to the taxi rank and went back to Sefton Park in my dressing gown and pyjamas.

19

Carole and I spent the next four months planning a future together and, by the middle of August, we decided to get married. But first I had to speak to my family in Iraq.

I was almost penniless, but an Iraqi friend in North Wales had told me of a faulty pay phone where you could phone anywhere in the world for free. We took a bus to Birkenhead, a train to Chester, another to Prestatyn, then a taxi to our final destination, where Carole stood guard outside while I told my brother Hamoud of our marriage plans. As we spoke, martial music played in the background.

'What's that music?'

'It's your favourite station, the *Voice of the People*: Iraq has just declared war on Iran! Don't worry, we've all made our choices and congratulations on yours!

'Look after your wife, have lots of kids and forget about Iraq. We're done for! Good luck!'

So it was that, eight months after our eyes first met in the lingerie department at C&A, Carole and I were married in the Liverpool registry office at West Derby Road on 3 September 1980.

With half an hour to go till the service only Carole had arrived. Tommy had locked the rest of the Harding family in the house. Only Jackie managed to escape, through the bathroom window, and my best man arrived with minutes to spare.

Before the service could begin the registrar warned Carole that, under Islamic law, I could marry up to four wives.

'That's alright, just as long as they don't all live with me!'

As we kissed and hugged after the ceremony the new Mrs Kadar whispered the immortal words, 'Welcome to Bedlam, love!'

20

Carole and I had been married about three months, living in a bedsit in Wallasey, when Tommy presented us with a bunch of keys.

'I've got you a lovely flat!'

It was in a new block: two bedrooms, central heating, goldplated taps and a marble kitchen – just what we needed, as we were expecting our first child.

All went well for the first couple of days, as we bought furniture and decorated a room for the baby, but on the third day there was a loud knock on the door. It was the council bailiffs telling us that this was not our flat: it belonged to the council and what were we doing here?

Tommy's 'gift' had been obtained, not with a mortgage, but by simply kicking the door down and calling in the decorators. One of the bailiffs handed me an envelope containing a letter telling us to vacate the premises immediately.

I slowly reread the letter, one word standing out that I hadn't seen before: 'squatter'. It sounded like the word 'wanker', which Tommy had introduced a year earlier, so I called him for a translation, man to man, and told him about our visit from the council bailiffs.

Within a couple of hours the flat was swarming with reporters. Tommy told Carole and me to sit on the sofa, put our arms around each other and look upset. Arabs, by nature, are a discreet race. To us, publicity is little more than veiled shame, so when I refused to pose for the cameras Tommy was outraged.

'This is how it's done in this country! Without the press on your side, you haven't a hope. You'll never get a new flat! Where do you think you're going to put the new baby, soft lad?'

Carole and I hugged each other on the sofa and the cameras flashed, while Tommy did all the talking. I guessed things might be getting out of hand when I heard him mention something about Wirral Housing Corporation '... and that evil bastard, Derek Darling.'

Next day, Carole and I were all over the front page of the *Liverpool Echo* with the headline: 'SQUATTER AND HIS PREGNANT WIFE EVICTED.'

First thing the following morning Derek Darling, Director of the Wirral Housing Corporation, was on the phone to Tommy and, within the hour, Tommy and I were in Derek Darling's office at Birkenhead Town Hall, its walls covered with honours and diplomas celebrating the man's unstoppable career.

After the initial introductions, Tommy launched into his assault.

'I can tell you all about the scams going on in Wallasey, and all the corruption, Mr Darling. Everybody hates you! They all think you're a c***!'

Sweat appeared on Mr Darling's brow as Tommy continued.

'... It's not me, Mr Darling, it's the others you should worry about. I mean, I'd never say anything rude about you, would I, Maji? Would I ever say anything about Mr Darling being a c***?'

I continued to stare at the wall, searching for any degrees I might have missed as Mr Darling, who had clearly had enough of Tommy's insults, replied, 'Look Mr Harding; enough of that bad language. Where council housing's concerned, you can't just walk in and help yourself.

'We have a system here in Birkenhead. In case you didn't know, it's called a "waiting list!"'

A brief pause, as Tommy smirked and made a limp-wristed gesture in my direction.

Looking up at the mock baroque chandelier, Mr Darling gathered his thoughts, then looked across the desk at Tommy.

'Look, I'll try to sort something out. It might take a few days, but it'll happen, believe me!'

Mr Darling then rose from his chair and walked us to the door. As he shook my hand, he put his hand on my shoulder and spoke quietly but firmly, 'Mr Kadar, you're a nice guy, but my advice to you is this: get out of Birkenhead as quickly as you can!'

Carole and I did indeed receive another set of keys: to a new flat in Birkenhead.

21

Unfortunately Tommy insisted on coming with us to view the new flat. It was immediately apparent that both lifts were broken, so we slowly made our way up the urine-soaked steps to the fifth floor.

'Bastards!' Tommy screamed, as he opened the door and led us into our new flat. 'Hey you, Jackie! Go down the paint shop, get two spray cans and bring them back here right away!'

As Jackie sashayed through the open door towards the staircase, Tommy leered, 'See her, that Jackie? She's a right sex carpet!'

Within minutes, she was back with two spray cans and, as Carole and I looked on in amazement, Tommy and Jackie went to war on the walls.

WOGS OUT – NO FUCKING ARABS – FUCK OFF – BLACK BASTARDS: lines and squiggles interspersed with script, so striking the flat looked like a modern art gallery.

By the time Tommy had finished spraying he was back at the front door telling us to stop what we were doing and leave immediately.

Outside Tommy carefully closed the front door, raised his foot, then put his boot straight through it, before tapping his nose and winking.

'Makes it look like a break-in, see! Don't worry; I'll get you a decent flat from those bastards. Only the best for my family!'

With that, Tommy took us downstairs to the phone box that stood by a grassy embankment to the right of the building.

Tommy tossed the used spray cans into the long grass, then went into the phone box. While I waited outside, Carole and Jackie left to join the rest of the family at Birkenhead market.

After making a few phone calls, Tommy took me back upstairs to the flat. Within a couple of hours every local hack and cameraman was there – the *Liverpool Daily Post*, the *Liverpool Echo*, *Granada Reports*, BBC Merseyside. Even the freebie papers were there.

Cameras flashed and journalists took notes as Tommy gave it his all, ranting on about the filth that was 41 Cleveland Gardens.

'Who do they think we are? Fucking monkeys?'

Tommy then led everyone back downstairs, past the broken lifts, and on to the grassy embankment by the phone box outside. He was mouthing off about local hooligans and how Mr Darling ignored his warnings about the local graffiti brigade, when one of the offending spray cans rolled slowly onto the pavement.

Tommy thought fast, pointing the journalists away from him and the offending can. 'See that lad there? He's come all the way from fucking Iraq!'

All eyes were now on me.

I glanced back at Tommy, now standing in front of the empty spray can, trying to back-heel it into the long grass. Each futile attempt was accompanied by a shouted headline.

'First we give his country to the fucking Jews!'

KERLINK!

'And now look at him. We can't even give him a decent fucking home!'

KERLUNK!

'Is this how we treat the fucking Arabs?'

KERLANK!

As the can cartwheeled into the long grass, Tommy came up with the biggest headline of his life.

'I want a maisonette in Wallasey! Not fucking Birkenhead! Wallasey! And I want it *now*, or I'll be on that phone to my shipmate, the fucking Duke of Edinburgh!'

A sharp intake of breath was followed by what can only be described as 'mass murmur', seasoned journalists looking up from their notepads and photographers frantically refocusing. Everyone scrambled for a closer look at this shipmate of the husband of Her Majesty The Queen: His Royal Highness, Prince Philip, 'the fucking Duke of Edinburgh'.

Carole and I were no longer the news story; Tommy was.

'I used to clean the Duke's car whenever he had a date with Lizzie, and he'd give me a tin of tobacco every time! Phil doesn't forget his mates, don't you worry about that! I'll get on the phone and tell him all about Maji's flat. The Duke'll have it sorted out in no time: just watch me!'

There was no going back now. The sea of journalists parted like a guard of honour on either side as Tommy strode towards the phone box.

He stepped inside, searching in his jacket pockets, then his trousers. Then he gingerly poked his head round the door, 'Anyone got the palace phone number?'

'Hang on a minute!' someone shouted, as she started leafing through her handbag. 'I've got it here!' She called it out to him.

We all looked on amazed as Tommy dialled the number, then looked back at the assembled throng and gave us the thumbs up. His face suddenly lit up, as he cleared his throat. 'My name is Tommy Harding and I want to speak to my shipmate, the Duke!'

After a minute or so of Tommy holding on, tapping the side of his nose and winking, he slowly put down the receiver and walked out to face his audience.

'He's fucked off for the day. What a bastard!'

Tommy really had served with HRH and liked him so much that, when finally court-martialled for trying to poison the entire ship's company, only Prince Philip had been spared Tommy's legendary 'Mio', the Mediterranean insect omelette.

22

Unemployment was the hallmark of Liverpool life in the early eighties, yet the spirit and humour of its people ensured that life was bearable.

Near our newly redecorated flat, past the boarded-up church, there was a youth club. It had table tennis and snooker tables – even a basketball court – but in reality the club was little more than a local drugs centre.

There were usually more youngsters standing around outside, drinking beer and smoking pot, than there were inside. Below, water seeped everywhere through rusting pipes and drains blocked by leaves and used condoms. The rubbish skip stood full to the brim with unwanted mattresses and headboards, a supermarket trolley balanced on top, its rusted wheels pointing forlornly to the sky. Across the road stood the drab shopping arcade with twisted wire shutters and, behind, towering above the arcade, was a Barclays Bank stationery depot, the whole place surrounded by barbed wire and security cameras. It was like a prison.

I was unemployed so I always had time to help Carole with the shopping. Only about four shops out of ten were open in the local arcade – the post office, where I cashed my dole cheque, the butcher, the betting shop and the pub. The rest, including the newsagent, hairdresser and launderette, had all been robbed so many times they'd been forced to close, the shop fronts now defiantly boarded up.

One day Carole asked me to buy three lamb chops. The butcher asked how much meat he should leave on each and, surprised, I jokingly replied, 'Would you like me to draw it for you?'

'Yes, please! Here's a pencil and paper.'

The butcher's stock was so low it was a wonder he managed to trade at all.

As I finished the drawing, he went over my outline with a felt tip pen, then trimmed and turned the chop exactly, before handing me three bones with a thumbnail of meat on each, in return for £3. You could get half a cow for that in Iraq!

To while away the hours I used to play Spot the Ball, a game introduced to me by Tommy. After I'd posted my entry, Carole and I would leave our dingy flat and drive over the Four Bridges to the Harding maisonette in Wallasey for entertainment.

If Tommy was bored, he'd put his record player by the window and play 'Colonel Bogey' at full blast, and whoever was passing would march in time to the music and salute as Tommy waved back, inviting them in for tea and a chat, and maybe even a game of cards.

Almost every time we went round there was a stranger having tea and toast in the sitting room, playing brag or pontoon with Tommy and the girls.

Tommy was always Banker.

A regular player was the local schools inspector, whose job it was to persuade young truants like Sandra, Carole's youngest sister, to return to school. By the time she agreed to talk to him he'd usually lost all his money playing pontoon with Tommy.

'Sandra, why don't you go to school?'

'I don't understand what they're talking about. It's just like going to a car boot sale, seeing nothing, then going back for another look! What's the point?'

The inspector soon gave up on Sandra. He just wanted to win his money back. But as long as Tommy was dealing his well-marked pack of Victorian nudes he'd no chance.

I remember a couple of fresh-faced Mormons, newly arrived from Salt Lake City, getting the Tommy treatment.

Hearing them speak with Miriam outside, he came to join them at the front door.

'Look boys, this is an open house. You're welcome to come in, provided you don't talk religion!'

This is a challenge no missionary can resist.

Tommy then produced his racing form book.

'This is *my* bible ... sex, alcohol and racing are all we talk about here!'

With that, he put the form book down on the card table and started shuffling the Victorian nudes, while Jackie offered the Mormons cigarettes and asked if they were still virgins.

Brenda told them about Billy, and how much she loved him.

Anxious to do their good work in what must have seemed like fertile ground, the missionaries started drinking Tommy's alcoholic fruit punch.

'It's nothing really, just a fruit drink!'

Two hours later two drunk Mormon teetotallers staggered out onto the street, not a dollar between them, and still two months to go before leaving this land of Sodom and Gomorrah.

23

One Sunday afternoon Tommy phoned Carole to tell her that Sandra was on her way to our Birkenhead flat to pick up the pie Carole had baked for him, but Sandra never showed up. I drove Carole to Tommy's and delivered the pie and there was still no news about Sandra.

The whole family was in a state, particularly Miriam. Tommy contacted the police and the press, and Sandra's details were printed in all the local papers. As Miriam became increasingly desperate she pleaded with me to help.

'People in Iraq light candles and float them in the river to bring back their missing loved ones. Why don't you try?'

'But what does it mean? How can a candle bring my Sandra back?' asked Miriam.

'There's a saint, al-Khidir, the saint of the water. You have to light a candle and place it in the river, then ask him from your heart for Sandra to return. They say it always works!'

Later that evening Miriam, the girls and I met at New Brighton, where the Mersey meets the Irish Sea, and soon dozens of candles were bobbing their way towards Belfast. Somehow their prayers reached Sandra in London and, a few days later, she turned up in Liverpool with an Arab boyfriend.

Hamid was instantly accepted by the family, for it was he who had returned their daughter, her dignity intact.

He had found her in Euston Station, with no money and nowhere to go, and although it took him nearly six months to persuade her to tell him who she was, he brought her back to Liverpool the day she did.

Eventually Sandra and Hamid went back to London, married and bought their own home in Docklands, but it wasn't a marriage made in heaven. Though Sandra lived as an Arab wife, she was still every bit a Harding girl, and Hamid could never fit in. He was too set in his ways. When the whole family gathered for Christmas lunch at their house in Docklands a few years later, Hamid's patience finally snapped. The Hardings were round the table performing the traditional family ritual – a game of cards complete with arguments, swearing, and disputes about Tommy's role as banker. It was too much for Hamid: as the host, he wanted a Christmas conference on family values, but no one was remotely interested.

After all this time, Hamid still could not understand what made this family tick: laughter, drama and beating the system. As Tommy made a move to collect his winnings Hamid, believing that Tommy was about to attack him, picked up a chair and waved it above his head, shouting, 'If anyone tries to leave I'll kill them!'

After a while, he agreed with the girls that Tommy could be released on medical grounds, as his heart had been giving him gyp for years. When Tommy got back to Liverpool early on Boxing Day morning he was on to Scotland Yard, and Docklands and Merseyside Police about an Arab terrorist who was holding his entire family hostage, and about to shoot them one by one.

At 3 pm that same afternoon armed police broke in through the front and back doors simultaneously, sub-machine guns aimed straight at Hamid's head. Two marksmen pinned him to the ground while the others checked the adjoining bedrooms. If it was hostages they were after, we were all huddled under the table with Hamid and his minders, playing bingo.

24

My skills as a textile designer meant little in the North-West, where the textile industry was already in its final stages of decline. Depressed and frustrated, I'd pass the time drinking coffee at the local Arab hangout, the Elham Restaurant in Renshaw Street, where I'd once worked as an impoverished student.

There I hoped to meet someone who might know somebody who might offer me some work, any work.

My chance came when I met a group of elderly Iraqis in the restaurant, all on a training course with the General Electric Company. All the young men were at the front, fighting the war with Iran, in those days.

The old boys could hardly speak a word of English and had never eaten anything like the food on offer at the factory canteen: sausages, chips, pasties and pies.

What they needed was someone who could offer *dolmas* and kebabs; someone with local knowledge who could be their translator, or trouble-shooter, perhaps.

I mentioned their problem to Carole, who suggested we invite them over for an Iraqi dinner the following night, which we did.

A couple of days later, while having coffee with them in the local Holiday Inn, the muzak suddenly stopped and the Tannoy rang out asking one of the Iraqis to come to reception immediately.

Alerting them that there was a message, the leader invited me to accompany him to translate.

This was my chance to prove myself as a translator of quality. Today Liverpool, tomorrow, *Insha' Allah*, the BBC World Service!

At the reception desk, the relaxed atmosphere had changed dramatically to something more threatening, and we found ourselves confronted by a furious-looking gentleman waving a copy of the *Liverpool Daily Post*.

'What do you know about this?' the man bellowed, holding up the front page with one hand and smacking the headline with the other.

'GEC FEEDS FOREIGN DELEGATION FISH & CHIPS!'

I looked at the headline, then the Iraqi elder, then back at the headline again.

'Go on, tell me! What do you know about this?'

'Nothing! Honestly!' I replied

'Who contacted the press, then? Ask your friend! Go on, ask him!'

The man nodded in the direction of the ancient Iraqis, but there was no need to translate.

The old boy understood immediately and replied in Arabic.

Yes, he had complained about the food at GEC, '... but only to my friends in the restaurant over a plate of houmous, and just this

Iraqi translator, not the newspaper.'

Our interrogator must have realised that the old Iraqi could never pull a stunt like this without foreign aid: there had to be somebody on the inside with local knowledge.

The GEC man's eyes narrowed as he wagged an accusing finger in my face.

'If you had *anything* to do with this *whatsoever* I'll make sure your embassy hears about it and you never work in this city again! Understood?'

With that, he threw the paper in the bin, turned on his heels and stormed out through the revolving door.

A few days later I saw Tommy and told him about my Iraqis and the newspaper headline.

'Good job you didn't tell them it was me, Maj,' he whispered, winking and tapping his nose. 'You don't know these bastards. They'd kill you for a pound!'

25

It was our wedding anniversary and we planned to celebrate at Tommy's favourite pub, The Dale. Tommy was keen to contribute, so when he heard that The Lamb was planning to celebrate Billy's birthday the same day, he suggested we combine the two.

Billy was married to Carole's eldest sister, and was king of The Lamb.

He held court there every day from opening till closing time, sitting at the same table always with a bottle of vodka, several pints of beer and a pile of ready-rolled joints in front of him.

For those who didn't like smoking or drinking, Brenda was his lady-in-waiting, offering slices of sweet-smelling, sticky brown cake.

We always knew when Billy was flying, because he'd head straight for the jukebox and, without even looking at the titles, press the same numbers again and again, before returning to his throne.

'Working Class Hero' was his anthem, the pool-cue his sceptre, and a battered old tweed cap his crown.

Occasionally he played pool, but mostly his cue stayed sheathed in its case by his side, ready to be brought down on the skull of anyone unwise enough to provoke him.

Despite the occasional outburst, the pub valued Billy's business: Billy *was* the business, so it was only natural that the landlord should offer The Lamb as the venue for Billy's birthday party. They would provide the cabaret; Billy would pay for the food and drinks.

Meanwhile Tommy paid for everything up the road at The Dale. He was the life and soul of the party, while Miriam stayed at home preparing pies, fish and chips and scouse, Liverpool's very own delicacy of mincemeat, ribs of fatty beef, lamb, potatoes, peas, onions and carrots served piping hot with slices of cold beetroot and buttered bread. All this was followed by Miriam's special rice pudding, and everyone left happy. Carole and the girls went home, while Tommy and I set off for The Lamb.

The place was packed. We struggled in through the door to see a stripper strutting her stuff in front of Billy and his pals. There was smoke everywhere. Joints and pints passed from hand to hand as the bright red spotlight followed her every move. We joined Billy building a stack of fifty-pence pieces on his table, as trays of bottles and glasses flew to and fro from bar to saloon, saloon to lounge and back again.

Seeing the cash, the stripper waggled her backside at the audience and, with a flourish, tore off her knickers and waved them at Billy. Then she danced towards us, picked up the first few coins from the pile of cash Billy had neatly arranged in front of her, before placing them delicately on a chair by the stage, without even using her hands. We were amazed, and Billy leapt on the stage to join her. As the crowd cheered, Billy passed her a joint, then suggested his idea of the perfect finale, if she wanted the rest of the money which was now piled high in six-inch columns on his table.

To more cheers, Billy escorted the stripper towards the bar and it was just as he was helping her straddle the Theakston's Old Peculier pump that the police burst in, ordered the work lights on and the pub cleared and closed immediately.

It was all too much for Billy. He launched into the middle of them and, bringing a chair crashing down on some poor policeman's head, shouted, 'Maj, quick, the cue! We only came to see one c*** and now I can see twenty of the bastards!'

I felt like a fully paid-up member of the Harding family.

26

My mother-in-law, Miriam, had only two dresses: one for wear and one for the wash. She was selfless to a fault, giving love and receiving ridicule in return, but ridicule is love of another form in the Harding family, something that took me many years to understand.

On our wedding day, Miriam put on her make-up and her spare dress ready to join us in the registry office, but Tommy disapproved of his daughter's choice and so locked Miriam in the lavatory just as the taxi arrived.

Miriam had been 'locked in the lavvy' all her life for, if she wasn't in the kitchen cooking or washing, she was hoovering, tidying or making beds, while the family watched TV. Tommy's insistence that the family should eat nothing but the best meant that she had to live on her wits to provide Welsh lamb, Angus steaks and Chinese takeaways on demand. Basic provisions, such as lard, vegetables and bread she'd buy from the local corner shop 'on tick'. The rest she'd pay for by selling junk at car boot sales. She'd never had a holiday in her life except, once, when she and Tommy visited their son, Alan, in Virginia. That ended in tears when she accused Tommy of having an affair with a woman called Miriam-Lou.

'That *hewer*, Miriam-Lou,' Miriam used to call her.

'See him, Maj?' she'd say, pointing at Tommy, 'He'd shag a fly, him!'

Miriam-Lou's name was on Miriam's lips almost till the day she died.

Carole and I had been living in London for about four years when Tommy telephoned with the news.

'That Miriam, she's dying.'

It was February. We packed our bags and drove as fast as we could to Liverpool, where Miriam had been diagnosed with cancer of the stomach earlier that day.

When we arrived, we were surprised how normal everything seemed to be: Tommy sitting on the sofa watching the racing while Miriam slaved away in the kitchen preparing dinner.

'See her, that four-eyed bastard? She thinks she's dying!'

'See that fat old bastard? He's driving me to an early grave!'

'Maj, she's a fucking liar! Ask her what she was doing at two o'clock this morning!'

We stayed a couple of nights and, with all the banter, the card games and the jokes, Miriam's illness was almost forgotten.

Back in London Tommy would telephone almost daily to update us on Miriam's condition. Only two weeks later he was on the phone expecting us to return to Liverpool.

As it turned out, Miriam was still cooking, cleaning and cursing Miriam-Lou, while Tommy was parked in his favourite sofa watching the racing.

It was as if neither had moved since we last saw them.

'Hey, you, four eyes! Where's the fucking tea, then?'

This was Tommy's way of assuring Miriam that life would go on as usual.

One afternoon, after we'd returned to London, Brenda called from the hospital to tell us that Miriam was now so seriously ill she might die at any moment.

As we drove up the M56, just past Runcorn, the sight that unfolded before us was even more spectacular than usual.

It was 5 June, the day after Miriam's birthday, and through a solitary gap in the brooding, black cloud, the sun's rays pointed to Arrowe Park Hospital, Frankby Cemetery and the surrounding hills.

I knew then this must be dear Miriam's last day on earth.

The ward where she lay dying was at the end of a long corridor but, before you reached the swing doors, there was an alcove with vending machines, telephones and seating for about forty.

The Harding family were there, all twenty of them, having a huge row.

Jackie had accused Tommy of mistreating Miriam for the past forty years, while Tommy blamed everyone else for not doing enough to help Miriam with the housework.

With Brenda taking the middle ground and blaming the GP, doctors and nursing staff for failing to diagnose Miriam's problems earlier, Tommy pointed to Carole every now and then to blame her for deserting her mother and moving to London.

Jackie rushed to Carole's defence.

'You and your *hewering* with Miriam-Lou. You should be ashamed of yourself!'

Tommy then stalked down the corridor, scratching his armpits and beating his chest.

'Nigger lover!' he shouted at Jackie, then, to anyone who cared to listen, 'It's her who should feel ashamed!'

Doctors and nurses hurried along the corridor looking busy, while Jackie blushed and bewildered visitors looked on. No one seemed to know or care about Miriam, whether she was conscious or unconscious, as Tommy paced up and down the corridor shouting, 'Who do you think we are? Fucking monkeys? Fuck off the lot of you bastards!'

Miriam died that evening with Tommy, all the children and grandchildren at her bedside still squabbling, but she wouldn't have wanted it any other way.

For the Hardings, even in death, life went on as usual.

After the funeral at St Paul's, where Paul the priest praised Miriam, her family and her wonderful cups of tea, we went on to Frankby Cemetery, where the seven daughters all carried Miriam's coffin to her grave.

There was a reception for the mourners in the church hall, where Tommy spoke of Miriam as if she were still by his side.

'Maj, that four-eyed bastard was a good woman.'

The reception over, Carole and I returned to the house to collect our bags. There, hanging on the kitchen door, was Miriam's floral pinny, which she'd worn every day I'd known her.

27

Finally, after two years, Mr Darling came up with a new property for Carole and me in Wallasey, just up the road from Tommy.

From then on, Tommy would take me with him wherever he went – to race meetings, political meetings, demonstrations and anything involving Mr Darling.

Through the small, barred bedroom window of our council maisonette, all was grey.

Rain drizzled down on frost-covered roofs, while opposite a sixties tower block cowered in the shadow of the massive concrete air vent that serves the Mersey Tunnel.

On the horizon, beyond Victorian flour mills, stand four swing bridges where ships once passed laden with Egyptian cotton, Iraqi dates and spices from the Yemen.

As Cammel Laird's steel smokestack spewed its grey fumes into a matching sky, I turned on the transistor for news of my country's war with Iran, the aerial pushing through a small crack in the rotting window frame, but there was no reception.

I set the dial to BBC Radio Merseyside: classical music from the Liverpool Philharmonic.

What was I doing here?

I heard my father's words of farewell echo in my head:

'See the house, the wooden bridge, the palm groves and the lemon tree and remember God is always with you.'

My father-in-law asked me if I wanted to see a politician from the House of Commons. 'There's a right lemon speaking at the Labour Club tonight!' he said.

It was a meeting with Labour MP, Gerald Kaufman, campaigning on behalf of Michael Foot as part of the run-up to the general election of 1983.

'I'll have that Jewish twat, Maj! You watch!'

While the Right Honourable member for Gorton stood on the stage predicting wonderful things for Wallasey after Labour's election win, I sat with Tommy in the front row, arms folded with three fingers raised towards the MP.

'Why three fingers, Tommy?' I whispered.

'Tradition, Maj. Whenever you see a Jew, give him the three fingers: "Who Killed Christ?"'

As Kaufman carried on about the future with Labour, Tommy's Welsh friend and fellow political agitator, Jack, leapt to his feet.

'Never mind that shite, Mr Kaufman; the Tories have already agreed to change the doors in every council house in Wallasey. What are *you* going to do, then?'

Before Mr Kaufman could reply, Jack carried on in his heavy, Welsh brogue:

'It's a disgrace, them doors stuffed with fucking egg boxes, fire hazards the lot of them!'

Kaufman seemed keen to respond, stuttering the word 'well' a couple of times, but Jack refused to give way, pointing me out to the MP for Gorton.

'See my mate here, Mr Kaufman? I've been to his country countless times. I've seen how lovely their houses are, how well their government looks after them!'

I thought Jack must be talking about Sweden or Holland.

'Which country does your *mate* come from?' Kaufman enquired, seeing my distinctly Arab features, but trying to sound conciliatory nonetheless.

'He's from Jordan! I drive my truck there all the time!'

Tommy and Jack's slogan was 'scandal brings publicity: publicity brings results.' It was crude, but highly entertaining.

A few weeks later, on election night, Tommy invited me to join him and Jack to watch the count at Wallasey Town Hall, which he was hoping Linda Chalker, the Conservative MP, would lose.

I parked the car while Tommy and Jack made their way inside. By the time I'd walked past the waiting policemen at the hall door, they were nowhere to be seen.

The count was well under way: the returning officer stood stiffly to attention, his chain of office glittering in the brightly-lit room, as the party candidates gathered on stage talking nervously to each other watching the count.

While savouring my first experience of democracy at work, I felt a tap on my shoulder, turned round and, instead of seeing Tommy or Jack, there was Derek Darling.

'Mr Kadar, what are you doing here? You're not supposed to be in the counting area: it's against the law.'

'I'm sorry, I was looking for Tommy.'

'He's up there in the gallery. By the way, we've got a new scheme for you! If you ever want to move out of Liverpool, come and see me. It's called the Mobility Scheme. I'd like to help you. I can get you a place in London.'

Margaret Thatcher's Conservatives, including Wallasey's local MP, Linda Chalker, romped home to win the election and Mr Darling was as good as his word.

28

Morale was low – with unemployment, the Falklands, the Iran-Iraq war and the Beirut hostages – but the biggest story in Liverpool was the imminent closure of the Cammell Laird shipyard in Birkenhead. I was eager to get close to the action.

Up to now, I'd always thought that British politics was a serious business, but Tommy and Jack had shown me the reality. How British politicians, the press and the public play the political game like a coconut-shy: from the smallest to the largest political stage, someone throws something at someone and the whole nation is entertained.

Tommy and Jack played for laughs at local level, telling each candidate what they expected in return for their vote, before revealing what had already been promised them by the rival parties. They acted almost like the President and Vice President of Wallasey, elected not by local voters, but by some higher power, to represent life's losers: council house dwellers, asylum seekers, gypsies, drug addicts, single mothers and, of course, the unemployed.

I joined Tommy at political rallies and picket lines and, in the process, met a trade union activist, later to become Deputy Prime Minister, John Prescott, but Tommy took an instant dislike to Prescott, like the unfortunate Gerald Kaufman, and decided to add his name to his 'hit list'.

No politician or political party was immune from Tommy's schemes; not even Her Majesty's Secretary of State for the Environment.

After the 1983 election, the regeneration of Liverpool was promoted as Michael Heseltine's personal project. Unemployment figures were down and the Toxteth riots seemed a distant memory, but little could Michael 'Tarzan' Heseltine have known quite what he was taking on when he confidently declared, 'I am here to learn from the people of Liverpool.' Tommy was more than happy to teach him.

At the time I drove a clapped-out Volkswagen Beetle. I had no driving licence, no exhaust, insurance or MOT, but I did have enough petrol to take us to Liverpool city centre and back.

After buying a length of chain and a padlock, I drove Tommy and Jack to the City Council railings near where Michael Heseltine was to plant a tree on Albert Dock. The occasion would mark the official launch of the second stage in the regeneration of Liverpool.

Tommy and Jack had both worked on Liverpool Docks and were deeply upset that their traditional way of life had been destroyed in the name of progress. They were determined that their protest should be seen and heard.

By the time we had parked the car, the city centre was packed with weekend shoppers, sightseers, buskers, people in wheelchairs and protesters carrying banners for and against redevelopment.

Seeing the size of our chain, a second group of Heseltine protesters made way, offering us their place by the railings.

Tommy and Jack stood together crucifixion-style, legs together, arms outstretched asking me to go easy with the chain. I began with Tommy: first his beer gut, then around his neck. An evil thought fleetingly crossed my mind but, with so many witnesses, I allowed him enough slack to breathe.

Then it was Jack's turn but, just as I finished, an old lady stormed out of the crowd towards us.

'It's people like you ruined Liverpool! You should be ashamed of yourselves!' she shouted. 'And you!' she screeched, looking at me, 'We don't want any more of you foreigners in Liverpool! Get back to Bangladesh, or wherever you come from!'

'Mind your own business!' I replied, pointing at Tommy; 'I'm with my father-in-law!'

Tommy winked back.

'That's right Maj. Take no notice of that old bag!'

The crowd warmed to this theatre of the absurd, as Jack weighed in.

'That foreigner's my mate, you old hag! And he's not from Bangladesh, he's from fucking Jordan! His government's nothing like ours; they look after them properly in Jordan. You should see their council houses. They're fucking lovely!'

Now it was time for Tommy to up the stakes.

'Where's that Tarzan? Why's he fucking hiding?'

There was a lull as the crowd looked up towards City Hall, from where Mr Heseltine was due to make his exit.

'Why doesn't he come out?' Cos he's a fucking coward! He can't face the truth. Look at Tate & Lyle over there. Fucking closed! All of you, what's wrong with you? Why don't you see? Look: Albert Dock over there! Fucking derelict!

'We used to make history once! Fucking great ships came to Liverpool and that's where we used to build them! Look, there's Cammel Laird! We made some of the greatest ships ever built there: the Titanic for starters, and where the fuck is it now?

'Bastards! And now they're going to sell the whole fucking shooting match, lock, stock and barrel! Who to? To the fucking chimps, that's who! Fucking bastards!

'And it doesn't end there! It gets fucking worse! Council doors made of fucking egg boxes! Bastards!'

Tommy's speech was confusing, spellbinding stuff. The pro-Heseltine lady had now joined a chorus of rowdy supporters chanting, 'Hooligan element, loonie left! Hooligan element, loonie left!'

It wasn't long before their chants finally got to Tommy.

'Fucking old hags! You need a good shagging, the lot of you!'

The crowd's attention was no longer on Tommy. It had turned towards the elegantly dressed Mr Heseltine as he trotted down the steps of the City Hall, waving to the crowd with one hand and running fingers through his golden locks with the other.

Jack was about to teach Mr Heseltine a lesson.

'We should be spending our money on fucking factories and houses with proper fucking doors, decent schools and hospital beds! Not fucking flower beds!

'Liverpool was once the greatest city in England! Cotton, tobacco, iron ... Our country's health and wealth all came through these fucking docks. We were masters of our destiny, but not now!

'Now you give us fucking trees to swing on! Do you think we're fucking monkeys, Mr Heseltine?'

Hezza and his entourage passed, giving us not a second glance.

Tommy beat his chest and roared like Tarzan: a last, desperate attempt to get the minister's attention to save the docks he loved, now lost forever.

He leaned against the railings exhausted, as Mr Heseltine reached the tree-planting site.

The Secretary of State planted his tree and the heavens opened.

The crowds ran for cover and Tommy reached towards me, like a dying man with a final request.

'Maj, go to Darling and give him the key to these fucking chains. Tell him Jack and I haven't eaten all fucking day, it's fucking freezing and pissing down. We are not fucking budging till he comes down here and unlocks us himself!'

Tommy urgently needed to make tomorrow's headline.

Driving back to Birkenhead, I paid the toll then a policeman waved me over.

'Your exhaust doesn't sound too clever, sir. Can I see your MOT?'

'No spik Engleze.'

'Can I see your driving licence, sir?'

I shook my head.

'You don't appear to have a tax disc.'

I shook my head again.

'How about insurance?'

'*Allah Kareem*!'

I got away with a note requesting me to produce my documents within the next three days. I reached Birkenhead Town Hall, walked into reception and asked to see Mr Darling immediately.

'You'll have to wait some time, sir. He's on holiday. He'll be back a week on Monday!'

I handed in the keys for Mr Darling as Tommy had instructed, left my car in the council car park and walked slowly back to Wallasey.

Tommy and Jack arrived late that evening angry, hungry and soaked to the bone.

'What happened to you and Darling, you bastard? You were supposed to come back and get us. Thank God for the fucking fire brigade!'

29

Within months of moving to our new flat in Notting Hill I found work as a textile designer and as a cab driver at weekends.

'Delta One Seven, Delta One Seven! I've got a "not quoted" for Euston! Interested?'

'Roger!'

'One bottle of Smirnoff, one carton pure orange juice, twenty Marlboro Lights and one pack of Durex Extra Safe, any flavour! White House Hotel, Euston Road, room 502. Urgent!'

This was not a job for me, not tonight. I refused.

My controller responded by insulting all callers and cutting them off dead, banging his head against the microphone, and begging Miriam and Jesus to intervene before pleading with me to reconsider.

This kind, gentle Irishman, self-educated, highly intelligent but excitable, was unable to understand that, if my parents were to discover that I delivered alcohol and condoms as a menial cab driver, they'd disown me on the spot.

'Give it to 31, the Professor!'

Osman, known as the Professor, was a Palestinian, the same age as me. He was the one who introduced me to his cab firm in north-west London.

For most Arab men, the route to success in England is usually measured in terms of academic and sexual performance. If an Arab can successfully complete a British degree in medicine or engineering so much the better, but to bed as many women as possible guarantees *al-khabir*, 'the expert', a special status on his return to the Middle East.

Women, particularly prostitutes, fascinated Osman and he would stay up all night to be the one to drive the French girls home at the end of their shift.

He charged the lowest possible fare in return for being allowed to eavesdrop on their stories *en route*.

Sometimes he'd even get invited in for coffee and *rafraîchissements horizontals*.

If you couldn't get Osman on the car radio by day, you could always find him in the French sauna, or Ladbrokes.

One day Osman got lucky and won £4,000 on the Grand National. Every cab driver in town was now Osman's friend, advising him how best to invest his winnings, but he only took advice from his 'girls'.

Eventually, like a true Arab, Osman chose the academic route as his starting point, investing all his money in an electronics degree at the Open University.

After his honours degree, money and sex would surely follow?

Four years on, Osman passed his degree with honours and

applied to become a theatre technician at London's oldest hospital, Barts, who were advertising for anyone who spoke reasonable English 'between 25 and 34; ethnic minority applicants welcome'.

Osman was the perfect candidate.

He became a theatre technician at Barts within the week and, only a month or two after, one of his regular fares, a prostitute known as Mercedes, spotted him in his white surgical coat outside the maternity ward.

He was talking loudly to a fellow technician about the delicate problems of one of his French sauna girls, Zizi.

On hearing Osman talk so volubly about her friend, Mercedes presumed Osman must be a gynaecologist, cabbing on the side to finance his gambling habit.

Soon, all the prostitutes of West London wanted an expert opinion from 'the Professor', in his cab if necessary, sparing them all the aggravation of the NHS: appointments, waiting lists, social security numbers, stirrups and, worst of all, men in bow ties.

Before long the racket coming from Osman's dark-tinted Volvo estate in-car surgery was the talk of Little Venice and Professor Osman al-Khabir the best-known, most highly respected cab driver in Maida Vale.

It couldn't last forever and, eventually, the Professor was betrayed.

Nobody knew for sure who did it, but when the hookers told their pimps, the Professor was on the first plane back to Palestine.

With his degree, the money and the girls, Osman returned to Gaza City a legend.

30

My cab was like my *diwan*, passengers talking politics, history, religion and, where women were concerned, affairs of the heart. For most Westerners, inviting a total stranger into their lives, for no matter how short a time, is anathema but, for Arabs, it is different. I took my passengers the Arab route, via Edgware Road, offering coffee and sweets along the way.

After everything I'd been through in Liverpool and London there was now regular work if I wanted it, and that work was offering me not just the freedom to choose where and when I worked but, more importantly, the opportunity to be *me*. I'd spent years trying to fit in and now I'd found a way of reconciling my past with my present and steering myself towards a meaningful future.

'Delta One Seven, One Seven . . . Pick up at the French sauna.'

I refused and turned on Spectrum Radio, London's multi-ethnic station, to find a heated debate in Arabic about the Iraqi revolution of 1958.

My controller interrupted, asking if I'd go to one of London's more exclusive addresses in Regent's Park, then take my passenger on to Knightsbridge, which I accepted.

He was the archetypal English gentleman, complete with bowler hat and umbrella, dark double-breasted suit, cream silk shirt and striped tie. He acknowledged me gracefully with a gentle nod, then climbed aboard and rested his fragile frame on the well-worn, torn velour that barely covered the back seat.

I turned down the volume on the rear speakers and carried on listening to the debate. It became more heated as a pro-monarchist guest poured scorn on Colonel Abdul-Kareem Kassem, leader of the revolution that resulted in the cold-blooded murder of the Iraqi royal family.

'That was the moment', the monarchist insisted, 'that Iraq entered the dark age from which she has yet to emerge.'

This was more than the republican participant could stand, who now proceeded to hail Kassem with a stream of glowing tributes.

Driving south down Baker Street, across Oxford Street to Grosvenor Square, listening intently as I turned west past the American Embassy and up towards Park Lane, something unusual happened. In a most resonant Iraqi accent my passenger quietly, and politely, asked if I was from Iraq. Surprised, I turned towards him and nodded, as he asked me to turn up the volume. Both of us now listened intently and, through the mirror, I saw him shake his head, exasperated.

'That's not true!' the old man exclaimed, 'You're probably not old enough to remember, but I was there ... it was terrible ... mob rule! The royal family all killed; the British Embassy sacked; some poor American torn limb from limb, and Prime Minister Nouri al-Said and Crown Prince Abdul-Illah strung up like meat in the street!'

Arriving in Knightsbridge and, upset by this account of a day my country had taught me to celebrate, I parked, turned off the radio, then turned to my guest, asking him to tell me more.

'You know, in those days, Iraq had more potential than half the countries in the Arab world put together. All the different groups were treated the same: Sunnis and Shi'ites, Christians and Jews, Kurds and Turks; even devil-worshippers got a look-in!

'The monarchy had everyone's interest at heart, but the people just threw it away!

'The Iraqi people must come to terms with the fact that, before they destroyed the monarchy, and the democratic way of life, they were doing rather well. Everything they have tried since has been a total disaster!'

The old man then asked me from which part of Iraq I came. Usually, I am vague and non-committal. Tonight, though, I felt different. I told him everything.

It was as if he had seen a ghost.

'My God! I knew your family well! I used to visit your region regularly at weekends. In fact, I well remember being a guest of honour once, with the Prince Regent, Abdul-Illah, in your uncle's house, Sheikh Mohammed al-Habib!'

The old man then leaned towards the passenger door. I quickly stepped outside to help him from the car, before warmly shaking his hand. Pressing a twenty-pound note into my palm, he strode purposefully up the steps to his mansion flat. He turned away from the old oak door with its stained glass and shining brass, his keys gesturing towards me.

'And if you should ever find out what happened inside the

palace, please let me know!'

   With the gentlest wave, he turned, pushed open the door and was gone.

31

It was 1992 and, in those days, politicians, prostitutes, film producers and drug pushers travelled in my cab.

Now we lived in London, I was close to the heart of British politics.

My crash course in Liverpool politics with Tommy and his Welsh friend, Jack, enabled me to blag my way to the Palace of Westminster to attend a charity lunch as a friend's 'business associate'.

It was ten in the morning as I left the barbers and went home to put on my grey double-breasted suit, designer tie and brown shoes that shone like burnished mahogany. All I needed now was my invitation.

By eleven, I was reversing the car, rehearsing my excuse for not having an invitation, when I saw one of my neighbours in the rear-view mirror running towards me.

She was waving something, like a small white flag. I carried on reversing and, as she got nearer, the view got clearer. It was an envelope: my invitation to the House of Lords delivered to the wrong door!

'Where are you going then, all suited and booted?'

'The House of Lords! Thank God you got it! I've been waiting for this almost all my life!'

And I had. It was the biggest day of my life.

My appointment to meet the noble lord was for drinks at 12.30 but, as I turned into the car park at midday, I realised I'd forgotten my wallet.

Here I was, penniless, about to enter the place where Lord Balfour had pledged Palestine to the Jews, where Suez was debated and, most important of all, Iraq's future would one day be decided, yet I didn't even have the money to buy a ticket for the car park.

With only one hour to go before the buffet lunch I had to think fast.

A few weeks earlier, I remembered, I'd eaten at a pizzeria up the road on Victoria Street. The manager was an Egyptian. Maybe he'd understand my predicament.

I rushed over to Victoria Street.

'Anyone want a taxi?' the manager shouted, when I explained my predicament.

By the time I returned to the House of Lords I was only ten minutes late for lunch.

I ran towards Chancellor's Gate, and, breathless and sweaty, introduced myself to the policeman on duty.

He looked me up and down then, moments later, a man appeared wearing a smart red coat.

'Mr Kadar. Kindly walk behind me at a slow pace until we reach the Cholmondeley Room, where I shall stop and so shall you. I shall then address His Lordship and His Lordship's guests and announce you. I shall then leave you there.'

I was impressed by his assuring words and gentle manner, but nothing had prepared me for what was to happen next.

As he pushed open the double doors, he stepped one pace forward then boomed out loudly, 'My Lords, ladies and gentlemen, Mr Maged Kadar!'

With my ears ringing, I shook hands with the noble lord. He looked exactly as I had imagined, with his lean, thin frame, pinstriped suit, and silk shirt with its stiff white collar.

He placed his left hand on my shoulder and told me of his meeting with the late Prince Abdul-Illah, Crown Prince of Iraq, on an official visit to Britain four decades earlier.

'Let me introduce you to some friends!'

As I mingled with his guests – a collection of bankers, stockbrokers and politicians – it slowly dawned on me that they were all here to talk business, not charity.

One suggested we meet for lunch to discuss business opportunities in Hungary. He must have thought I was the son of President Kadar! Another, from American Express, suggested I move up to the gold card to cover the £8,000 I already owed on my green one.

Later, as His Lordship and I sipped champagne and nibbled anchovy toast on the terrace, it seemed the perfect moment to mention my starving people in Iraq.

Maybe he could help.

No sooner had we started discussing the problems facing Iraq than his words were drowned out by the sound of a passing barge.

Through it all I nodded sagely, 'Yes, of course ... Oh, yes ... That's right ... Oh, absolutely!'

Then, after the barge had passed, I asked him if he remembered the revolution.

'I remember it well ... Bastille Day, Monday, 14 July 1958. The King, Queen Mother and almost your entire royal family murdered.

Things are better now, aren't they, Mr Kadar?'

'Well, I was only one at the time but, as I understand it, that was when forty years of frustration with the British finally boiled over. The Arabs still blame them for everything that's gone wrong since!'

His Lordship seemed to take my remarks in his stride.

'My dear fellow, not just the Arabs!'

'Who else?'

'Well, the French, for starters. They're the reason we keep the bomb, but don't tell anyone!'

We laughed, and the reserve I'd felt when I first arrived melted away.

'Arabs may have their quarrels with the British but they don't rate the French much either! The Sykes-Picot Agreement gets them going just as much as the McMahon-Hussein correspondence and, as for the Balfour Declaration! Well, Arabs have been waiting for a steward's enquiry ever since.

'The list is endless but what really hurts is how you set Arab against Arab from the moment you first set foot in the Middle East.'

By now we were back in the Cholmondley Room and his Lordship beckoned me to join him on a green leather sofa.

'The truth is that the Arabs *do* have plenty of grounds for complaint, but you have to understand that everything the British and French did in those days was for stability and order, to maintain the balance of power.'

I realised that this was a former diplomat no longer restricted by convention, eager to offer his own steward's enquiry for my benefit, and mine alone.

'It sounds simple, but it's all rather complex; we had to make sure that no one was more powerful than anyone else and that everyone had enough to go round ... not too much and not too little; the rights of the individual taking precedence over the rights of individual nations and the powers that be.

'You have to understand that with the fall of the Ottoman Empire and the new world order that emerged after the Great War, we honestly believed that a dose of democracy was what you chaps wanted.

'It never dawned on us that Arabs might prefer some powerful, unelected leader, answerable to no one!

'With all that oil, we had to put our own people in charge to avoid trouble and keep things simple but, by creating those new borders, we caused more problems than we solved. It was madness!

'We were so busy thinking about the people, giving them new hope, new land and everything that came with it – education, hospitals, infrastructure and so on – we forgot that camels had been using the same routes and feeding grounds for hundreds of years and as far as they were concerned, the new borders were a load of poppycock from day one!

'We built barriers and border posts to stop them getting

through, but camels don't recognise flags and demarcation lines!

'It's a juggling act trying to find the balance between borders and resources and, inevitably, you're going to get it wrong somewhere and make enemies.'

It was hard to take in all my host had to say, but harder still when the waitress returned with more vol-au-vents and cocktail sausages, while another poured champagne. His Lordship gave a knowing wink, just like Tommy would have done.

'And I'll tell you another thing, my friend. By denying Iraq a proper seaport, just to create a tiny state like Kuwait, is a mistake we'll be paying for for a long time to come!

Creating countries out of mere counties was a disaster; like turning Rutland into a republic!'

A burst of shared, spontaneous laughter and I could feel the bond between us growing.

'You're right. The British thought that by cutting us off from the sea they'd make us lightweights in the region. Well, there they were always going to be wrong.

I remember how excited people used to get when they spoke of Kassem's attempt to take Kuwait in 1960. When the British finally left, they came back to block us.

What they did when Saddam eventually crossed the border in 1990 is still going on as we speak: they took back Kuwait and they are now systematically destroying what's left of us.'

There was a sharp intake of breath before he responded.

'I assume you mean the sanctions and the bombing. Do you think there's an alternative?'

'Yes. First of all, people must recognise that we Iraqis are people like them. We need to eat in order to live and behave rationally.

We are not children. Treat us like children and we will act like children: we shout, scream, spit and kick, and if it goes on like this, soon you'll find yourselves fighting *real* children. But treat us like adults and we will respect you in return. And in time you might learn to respect us.'

A quiet cough, followed by a gentle tap on my shoulder.

'Friend, everything you say shames me, because I recognise that what you tell me is the truth. What we British have done to your country from the beginning is nothing short of tragic.

'We gave you a monarchy you didn't want, a parliament that didn't work and now we're bombing the living daylights out of you. No wonder you're upset!

'I know Iraqis are a proud people and, as for that Saddam, he's a legend.

'To continue worrying the hell out of the West with his weapons of mass destruction, whether real or imagined, is immaterial.

'He has created a classic stalemate from which only he can emerge the winner, dead or alive.

'Look at the options. We can either carry on bombing and wait for Saddam to die, or invade Iraq and remove him by force.

'If that happens, we'll put another puppet in power, watch him get shot, then we're back where we started. Whatever happens, whether Saddam lives or dies, he's already a legend.

'If, on the other hand, sanctions are lifted and conciliatory efforts are made between Iraq and the West, Saddam will continue as a legend; the world's great survivor.

'Whichever way it goes, this is one battle Saddam can't lose and the West can never win!'

I could hardly believe what I was hearing, and felt honour-bound to match honesty with honesty.

'Iraqis are a proud people, like you British, but we are different in one way: ideas excite us much more than facts; words and poetry excite us even more, and that's why we've achieved so little and our future is so uncertain!'

There was a brief silence, as His Lordship turned towards me and clasped my hand.

'Look, the Americans run the world now. There's nothing I can do for you that'll change a damn thing!'

Saddam had invaded Kuwait two years earlier and my visit to the House of Lords had done little to allay my fears for my family in Iraq. Family life in England, too, was starting to feel the strain.

32

Seven years after my trip to the House of Lords Iraq was still in a state of war, my relationship with my wife and children was at its lowest point and, for the past two days and nights, British and American bombing had turned Baghdad into a city of flames.

For the first time since I'd come to England, the seasons of Christmas and Ramadan coincided.

Saddam's challenge to the United Nations to lift their embargo before UN personnel could be readmitted into Iraq to search for WMD had been answered by war, not words.

I was tired, angry and desperately worried about my family in Iraq. I imagined them hiding somewhere in the ruins of Baghdad without food, electricity or warmth, while I sat with Carole and the children watching *Neighbours* or *Friends*.

Quite apart from having only soiled flour for food, my brother Hamed had written to say that he and his wife and five children were about to be evicted from their home because they couldn't afford the £500 to buy the house outright.

I pleaded with Carole to send some of our Christmas savings back to Iraq but, no matter how hard I tried to explain, her reply was pure Marie-Antoinette:

'They should eat *baklava*!'

We filled our plates from a table piled high with assorted meats, stuffed vegetables, salads, fruit, dates, nuts, crisps, After Eights and the obligatory mince pies.

I took my first bite of rib-eye steak as Kylie, Jason and the stars of *Neighbours* tucked into theirs by the pool. Then I threw my plate across the table, leaving a trail of steak, chicken and vegetables all over the floor.

Carole and the children froze. They'd never seen me act this way before.

Little did they know that my head and heart were in turmoil. The argument with Carole, my brother's letter from Iraq and now the bombing in Baghdad were more than I could handle.

I noticed an empty box of Mr Kipling mince pies while wiping the mess from the floor. The words of Rudyard Kipling swirled round my head: 'East is East, and West is West, and never the twain shall meet!'

Carole and I were East and West, two different worlds; apart, separate and unique. We would never be one if we continued like this, not caring, not listening, not trying to understand one another. I dreamed of a day when we could accept our differences, celebrate them and rebuild our relationship around them.

33

March 2000. Little more than a year had passed since Clinton and Blair's four-day bombing campaign of Iraq on behalf of the United Nations. Sporadic attacks, in response to Saddam's refusal to allow UN weapons inspectors to stay on in Iraq, continued around the 'no fly zones'.

It was hard trying to make sense of my life, without being able to see for myself what was going on in Iraq. Reading the Iraqi press and watching satellite television it seemed fairly clear that, as far as Saddam was concerned, he had already honoured his side of the deal with the United Nations. Iraq's weapons of mass destruction had been destroyed, so there was nothing left to discover.

After ten years of almost total embargo, the Iraqi people had suffered enough: it was now time for the UN to lift the sanctions.

Unfortunately, Saddam's agenda was not accepted and was not getting any coverage in the British press.

Without the opportunity to check every grain of Iraqi sand, Britain and America still insisted that Saddam possessed WMD, a serious threat to world peace.

The only way I got through all this was by losing myself totally in football.

For ten years football had been my passion – not just mine, but the whole family's. Every Saturday and Sunday morning, we would pack a picnic hamper with soup, sandwiches and a flask of tea, before Abbas, Jasim and I would drive all over Surrey in our quest for football glory.

Each week, rumours would fly: which scout from which football club would be watching where.

Every ground we'd visit was surrounded by trees and streams, something my family in Iraq could never have imagined, particularly now, with the cherry blossom a mass of pink and white and daffodils with their yellow trumpets announcing the start of spring.

Looking up from the muddy playing fields, a plane banked above as if for a better view of the free kick Abbas was about to take.

How much longer would I have to wait before being allowed to fly back to Baghdad?

At that moment, the plane disappeared into the midday sun, Abbas and his teammates celebrated and I felt a twinge of hope that my twenty-year absence from Iraq was about to end.

The next morning, as I flicked through the mail, a white envelope caught my eye with its distinctive rubber stamp: 'The Hashemite Kingdom of Jordan'.

I tore open the letter.

Dear Mr and Mrs Kadar,
We have the honour to invite you to visit your homeland, meet

your family and friends and see at first hand the suffering of your people inflicted by the enemies of peace.

You will be attending a conference hosted by His Excellency, President Saddam Hussein. You will be invited to visit hospitals, colleges and museums on official tours. You will also have the opportunity to walk freely amongst the people and hear their views.

During the conference you will be staying at a five-star hotel, all expenses paid. However, any donations, literature and medical supplies will be much appreciated.

Whatever your profession, you will be given the opportunity to give a lecture on your subject: this will be your opportunity to show solidarity with your own people and help break the sanctions in the process.

You can call during office hours to arrange the formalities.

Signed,

Dr Muadhfar Amin,

Iraqi Chargé d'Affaires, London

My first thought was 'Is this a trap?' Then, 'My God! Carole's been invited to Iraq by Saddam Hussein!' before remembering her views on the subject ('I'm not going *anywhere* where Scud missiles are flying over my head!')

My decision was made. I would return to Iraq on my own as the President's guest and, after the formalities were over, look Saddam firmly in the eye and advise him, as a London cab driver, that he should take a completely new route and start again.

Saddam is so grateful, he appoints me his Foreign Minister, adviser or even roving ambassador. I accept with humility whichever role he has in mind and, with reluctance, whatever perks might come with the job.

The pressure was getting to me.

On the way to Heathrow, I asked Carole if she'd remembered the £100 she'd promised me.

'We'll get it at the airport.'

All my unspoken fears of what might happen in Iraq poured out of me like a burst water pipe.

I was returning to Iraq for the first time in twenty years with just £200, blaming Carole for everything that was wrong with our lives.

By the time we got to the airport and said our goodbyes, I knew that, by leaving without her, Abbas and Jasim, I risked losing them forever.

34

I arrived at Amman Airport in the early evening, desperate to get to Iraq as quickly as possible – not only to meet my family after twenty years away but to phone Carole and make peace.

On the way to al-Kut where the family now lived, I phoned from the border to tell them I was on my way and would be arriving later that afternoon.

As we turned down the dusty, broken street littered with bricks and broken bottles, black sewage zig-zagged along the middle of the road.

James Baker had certainly made good his promise 'to bomb Iraq back to the Middle Ages' and Fairouz would have turned in his grave to see his clean streets looking more like rubbish tips.

The polished cars and minibuses that once travelled up and down the tarmac streets were now replaced by donkey carts, their drivers reduced to selling vegetables and cooking oil.

Once a place of beauty, al-Kut's perfumed streets had been lined with palm, lemon and fig trees. Now the trees were gone, the whole city engulfed by the stench of raw sewage.

Here the family house still stood, but everything around it had shrivelled and died.

Despite all the decay, the whole neighbourhood lined the crumbling road to greet me. The heat, the stench and the emotion overwhelmed me as I stepped from the car, spotted my mother at the doorway and headed towards her, but the crowd had other ideas.

Brothers, nephews, nieces and people I'd never even met hugged, held and kissed me and, before I could say anything, I found myself carried on a tide of humanity laughing, crying and clapping as they pushed me towards the *diwan*.

It looked much smaller than I remembered. The one at al-Moraibi held about eighty people on cushions and carpets but here, in the city, there was only room for forty: twenty on the carpet and about another twenty on sofas and armchairs.

There was a cabinet in the centre packed with religious books and, on the bottom shelf, a telephone surrounded by all the tools for making coffee.

The only thing missing from the old days was the *magsala*, replaced now with a stained ceramic sink by Shanks of England.

Otherwise, little had changed, or so I thought, until my father appeared, his wrinkled skin and wispy, long beard giving him the appearance of a hermit emerging from some other age.

As I approached, his legs gave way, but I caught him as he fell and, gently, helped him to the ground and together, there on the floor we hugged, his head resting on my shoulder as he whispered, sobbing, 'I was afraid I might die before I saw you.'

I told him that I had always known we would meet again and it was this that had kept me going all these years.

This seemed to reassure him and, as we sat down on the sofa, I reminded him of how he had listed everything I should remember the last time we were together. I told him how he'd asked me to remember the house, the bridge, the palm groves, the lemon tree, the people in the village, their generosity and how God would always be with me. I asked him when he had seen al-Moraibi last. He smiled and squeezed my hand. The house in al-Moraibi was now little more than a shell since the drought. The village had been boarded up and shuttered for almost ten years since Saddam cut off the water supply to the south.

This was his revenge for the Shi'ite uprising in 1991, when President Bush urged Iraqis to rise up and oust him. Now the whole of al-Moraibi was like that dead piece of earth in my dream where nothing grew. There was no more water and no more fish. Even the old kiln that had shaped so many childhood memories had now crumbled into dust.

My mother still had her shuttle but her worries now were not about feeding my father's guests, but how to ensure my safe return from Saddam's conference. She stood aside as we ate, watching proudly like a mother hen, her brood back together at last. With all the visitors and well-wishers, my mother and I had struggled to share more than a few moments together, but now we could sit and talk at length for the first time.

'I wish Carole and the children were here,' she said quietly, 'and I pray that one day, God willing, they *will* come so we can celebrate as one big family.'

35

Baghdad was drier than al-Kut, despite the opulence of the al-Rasheed Hotel where hundreds of Iraqi expatriates now gathered at the Palace of Conferences to hear the opening speech of Tariq Aziz, Saddam's deputy.

After the usual opening rhetoric he produced a box of matches from his jacket, held it up and declared:

'Ladies and gentlemen, *these* are the weapons of mass destruction that they're looking for! (*Shakes match box.*)

'According to them, this is a dual-use weapon! I can light my cigarette with it, but they insist I can also use it to burn half the world! (*Shakes match box.*)

'These sanctions are so unnecessary! They're killing men, women, children, the weak, the sick and, to compound the problem, they're using it to sell what they can't sell to the world: out-of-date food and medicine!

'To them, we're no more than a business deal!

'Ten years of sanctions, half a million dead as a result and they *still* insist they're not going to lift the sanctions till we remove these weapons of mass destruction! (*Again, shakes match box.*)

'They preach to us about democracy and fairness! Believe me, worse is to come! They will attack us again, but we will be there to meet them.

'We won't be defeated!'

The atmosphere was now positively supercharged as the chairman of the conference proposed the setting up of committees around the world to promote Iraq's cause abroad. The committees would be divided into various groups, including health and medicine, science, media, trade and economics.

Everybody signed up – doctors, scientists, academics, lawyers, artists, traders and musicians. Every walk of life seemed to be represented, except cab drivers.

What could I contribute?

I attended four more presentations with various ministers: the Foreign Minister, al-Sahaf, later known as Comical Ali, the Trade Minister, the Transport Minister and the Information Minister.

First up was al-Sahaf, who arrived four hours late, congratulated us on our success, then admitted he knew nothing about what we'd been discussing, but confidently declared, 'I understand that whatever you *have* been discussing has been going rather well!'

Afterwards, I walked up to the podium, shook his hand and requested a short meeting to ask what I could do to promote Iraq's cause in Britain. Al-Sahaf thanked me for my support, but told me he had urgent business to attend to in Amman.

The other ministers, too, were all too busy to see me but, apparently, grateful for my support.

As a last desperate throw of the dice, I decided to try my luck at the Baghdad School of Fine Art. If I was lucky, I might yet introduce them to the Tommy Harding School of Politics.

About forty students and teachers gathered round as I opened with a brief summary of where Iraq had gone wrong in the eyes of the rest of the world.

With all eyes fixed on my delegate's badge, MAGED KADAR – UK REPRESENTATIVE, I suggested that Iraqis should recognise that things were not okay; that it was time for us all as a people to admit to the errors of our ways and face up to our responsibilities.

'We must own up to the fact that we ourselves are responsible for our current state. Unless we repair our ways, there is no way out of the current crisis.'

It was when I suggested that the Iran-Iraq war was viewed in England as a waste of time and life that the mood changed and, by the time I started discussing the Kuwait issue, the interruptions began. Some were polite, but a teacher in her fifties took grave exception to my remarks, and for good reason.

'You were in England during the Iran-Iraq war, so you can't possibly know.

'Are you telling me that my husband died in that war for nothing?

'And what about the Kuwait war? Where were you when Um Ghaida lost nine of her children in the al-Amiriya shelter. You should meet her!'

The following day I was introduced to Um Ghaida in the same air raid shelter in which her children had met their deaths, and which she now made her home.

The congealed, dry skin of the dead still remained embedded on concrete pillars; highlighted all the more by the charred walls resulting from the fireball that engulfed the entire building over a decade earlier.

Wearing a simple black dress and a silver pendant round her neck, Um Ghaida was a picture of grace as she pointed her torch towards the spot where she had left her nine children that night. Some were sleeping, others playing while, way back towards the furthest wall, a group of friends and neighbours sat talking.

She described how she had returned to her house over the road with her youngest son who refused to stay in the shelter, preferring to help her bring in the washing.

It was around midnight.

Then, with a terrible roar, a Cruise missile turned down her street, diving down the ventilation shaft, the explosion that followed rocking the whole city.

Wiping away tears, Um Ghaida continued:

'There was no distinction. Everyone was incinerated in a single moment.'

Her voice slowly gained strength as she pointed her torch towards the grisly scene around us.

'We've given up on the West having pity on us; they are so far removed from our predicament we can't expect anything from them, but what about our Arab brothers? They should at least feel for us, but they're even worse than the West. They allow the Americans to attack us from their own countries so they can hang on to their thrones!

'That's what you should tell people in England. You were brought up here. This is your country. You were educated here. It's the least you should do.

'Why aren't there any demonstrations supporting the Iraqi people?

'We're a nation under siege yet, in America last week, the whole nation demonstrated to get one little boy returned to his father in Cuba!

'I'm happy for the little boy, but why is the world so silent about us?

'You have seen for yourself. Now tell the world what you've seen!

'Don't just worry about yourself. You'll live, believe me, even if you just sell water!

'Why suffer estrangement and prejudice in another land if you have nothing to show for it?

'Now is your chance to do something meaningful! Take this picture with you: not just of the shelter, but of an entire nation.

'Lift the sanctions! This is your mission! This is my hope in you! If you want me to stop wearing this black dress, if you want me to smile again, tell your people about our tragedy!'

I arrived at Heathrow the next day, with Um Ghaida's picture.

36

Getting the media involved might have been a job for Tommy but I was too ashamed to ask for his help. I'd left Carole soon after my return and, besides, Tommy was now just a shadow of his old self, in and out of hospital.

He died a few weeks later and, just like Miriam before him, the family was arguing about his will before he was even cold.

Without Carole, the children, Miriam and now Tommy, I felt more alone than at any point in my life and decided I should go back to Iraq to spend some time with my parents before I lost them too.

Living on my own I had managed to save some money and I borrowed another £5,000 to leave in the bank for Carole and the children.

I flew to Damascus, then on to Baghdad and straight to the family home in al-Kut. It was as if I had never been away, and my mother and father picked up from where we'd left off almost a year earlier.

My father was in good health and good spirits, so good he wanted to take the whole family back to see the house in al-Moraibi.

The next morning we gathered in the garden ready to make the journey to the village, when my father saw some crumbs on the grass. The idea of throwing food away was, to my father, *haram*, a non-permissible act, and I watched as he bent down to pick them up piece by piece.

Very slowly, he rolled onto his side and, as I ran up to help, I noticed that all the colour had drained from his face.

We carried him across the garden to the *diwan* and laid him down in that same corner by the window where he would eat, entertain and pray. While we waited for the doctor, he asked me to sit with him:

'Son, it may be God's will that we can't go to al-Moraibi today. I wanted to take you. There are many people who I would like you to meet but, God willing, you'll have the chance to meet them another day.'

My father died a few days later and, at his funeral the following day, I met all the people he had wanted me to meet – old friends from al-Moraibi who I hadn't seen for thirty years; followers and friends from all over the south; even Saddam's representative from the local Ba'ath Party.

The city of al-Kut was closed. Tens of thousands came to say goodbye. After prayers in the mosque, poems and speeches were read celebrating his life, before we carried his coffin through the city wrapped in the same silk flag that had flown above the family *diwan* since before I was born.

We surged past the Ba'ath Party office chanting even louder, as my father's coffin rested on the fingertips of hundreds of his followers, as if floating to his final resting place.

A few days earlier he had told me, 'I owe God money for what's left of the year.' It was $800.

Besides my return ticket I had $4,000 left: $800 to pay the charities and needy families, with $3,200 left to feed seven thousand mourners over the next seven days.

Everything that had happened in my life up to this point – Iraq, England, the Hardings, Carole, Abbas, Jasim, the taunts, the tears, the laughter; everything – for the first time, all the sights, sounds and emotions I'd seen, heard and felt now had meaning.

My father, al-Sayed Mousa Khedhir al-Hammashe, had died on 31 December 2001, the very day his debt to God was due.

37

I arrived back at Heathrow penniless and made a collect call to Carole.

She was watching *Brookside*, so I asked if Abbas could pick me up instead.

'He's just come back from Uni and says he's tired.'

I pleaded for them to come and pick me up, as I had no money and didn't know where to go.

After three months away, it was as if I was coming to England for the first time: a new me meeting a new Harding family.

When the car drew up, Abbas got out, shook my hand and ushered me into the back seat while Carole sat silently in the front without giving me so much as a glance.

The music blared and not a word was spoken while I asked myself what God might have in mind for us all.

'Have you got somewhere to stay?'

'No, I've spent everything on my father's funeral.'

'That's all you care about, your family in Iraq!'

There was no point arguing.

Carole put a mattress on the floor and, after she and Abbas had gone to bed, I lay awake deep in thought.

I had tried to interest my Iraqi family with my Western view of life, but it had meant nothing to them, because it had no connection with their Arab reality and, similarly, during my time in England I had tried many times to introduce the Arab view of life to Carole and my children, but failed for the very same reason.

My trip to Iraq had shown me the importance of both my families, yet neither seemed willing or able to relate to my 'other' self, that other world in which I also resided. They only related to my world as they knew and understood it; anything beyond that boundary seemed beyond them.

Slowly, I realised that in order to express the love I had for both my families I would have to do it on their terms and, in order to truly express that love, sacrifice the 'other' me, losing the self that alienates me from them, East from West, and vice versa.

The following morning I returned to my old cab office in Maida Vale.

'Where have you been, Maged? Haven't seen you for ages!'

My Irish controller seemed pleased to see me back. He was my one and only hope to get me back on my feet, back on the road.

'I need a car.'

'There's a red Volvo Estate round the back. You can have it for fifty quid a week, but nobody's driven it since the Professor!'

'I'll take it. Can I pay you in a couple of days?'

By lunchtime, I'd earned enough to pay a week's deposit for a room in Isleworth.

It is now three years since I left Carole and the family. I have my own cab and as I sit eating my sandwich listening to the radio in Richmond Park, they play a track Carole and I used to sing when we were together, 'We Can Work It Out'.

Halfway through, the music fades, 'We interrupt this programme to bring you a news flash: Saddam Hussein has been captured!'

I gaze through the rear view mirror, beyond the battered interior of my ageing cab, the torn seat covers and cigarette burns that pepper its plastic upholstery, to see something more ... much more.

Stags leap on tiptoe as if dancing the Chobi, the traditional dance of Baghdad, and, for the first time in years, I am finally at peace with myself and my world. But then I see Carole's picture on the dashboard and the heart-wrenching pain returns.

Afterword

Since about 4000 BC, Iraq has come under the influence of nine different cultures: first, the Sumerians, then the Babylonians and the Assyrians. Later, the Persians, the Greeks, the Arabs, the Turks, the British and, finally, the Americans have all attempted to rule this unruly land.

The world owes much to the Sumerians, who discovered not only the written word, but also the mathematical concepts of zero and the division of time and space into multiples of sixty. The Sumerians are also responsible for the discovery of that intoxicating substance they named *al-cohol*.

The Babylonians followed, giving Iraq and the world something of even greater importance than buildings and gardens: the Code of Hammurabi, guaranteeing the Rights of Man, 'So that the strong may not oppress the weak.'

The Persian King, Cyrus the Great, followed the Assyrians, invading Mesopotamia in 549 BC.

He developed a taste for alcohol, the 'elixir of life', as did

Alexander the Great, who defeated the Persians in 331 BC, introducing a period of Hellenistic influence that was to last two hundred years until the return of the Persians, finally overcome in their turn by the great Arab invasion of the seventh century AD, bringing with it the new message of Islam.

By the tenth century, with the Abbasid dynasty established almost two hundred years, Baghdad had become the capital of an Islamic Caliphate that extended westwards from Samarkand in Central Asia to the Moroccan shores of the Atlantic, and from the gates of Constantinople in the north to Sudan in the South.

Both the Islamic Caliphate and the Abbasid dynasty came to an end with the Mongol invasion of Baghdad in 1258 and, by the mid-sixteenth century, the whole of today's Iraq had come under Turkish rule, the two Islamic cultures coming together as part of the Ottoman Empire until the arrival of British troops in 1917.

This time, however, Iraq possessed a new, more precious 'elixir' than alcohol: oil.

The modern state of Iraq was established by the British in 1920 in the aftermath of the First World War through the reunification of three provinces of the defeated Ottoman Empire – Mosul on the northern border with Turkey, Baghdad in the centre and Basra to the south – but Iraq's problems with Britain began almost as soon as the British troops arrived in March 1917, after a deal between al-Sharif Hussein, Custodian of the two Holy Shrines of Mecca and Medina, and Sir Henry McMahon, the British High Commissioner in Egypt.

The McMahon-Hussein correspondence of 1915–16 had been interpreted by the Arabs as a promise to their leader, al-Sharif Hussein, of Britain's future support in the reconstruction of that ancient Islamic Caliphate of the eighth century in return for continued Arab cooperation throughout the Middle East.

The borders of the proposed new kingdom would extend from Greater Syria in the north to the northern part of the Arabian peninsula in the south, and from Persia in the east westwards right up to the Mediterranean shores of Palestine.

However, the Balfour Declaration of 1917 guaranteed the Jewish people a 'national home' of their own in Palestine, then a country with a ninety per cent Arab population, meaning that the western portion of the proposed new Arab kingdom was now guaranteed to a second party who formed only ten per cent of the population.

Worse was to follow.

Britain, torn between two apparently irreconcilable promises to both the Arabs and the Jews, was further embarrassed when secret documents came to light in the wake of the Bolshevik Revolution of October 1917.

The secret Sykes-Picot Agreement between the British and the French was to come into effect when hostilities ceased, taking full advantage of the vacuum left by the defeated Turks, the two allies splitting the Middle East heartland north of the Arabian peninsula into two spheres of influence.

The French would take Lebanon and a greatly reduced Syria, with Britain taking what was left of Greater Syria, Palestine and Iraq under direct British rule. The area later to be known as Transjordan would become a British Protectorate.

This meant that at the end of the war, instead of creating a new Islamic state as a quid pro quo for siding with Britain and France, the Arab leader, al-Sharif Hussein, was to get nothing and, after the war, was driven out of the Arabian peninsula by Britain's other chief Arab ally, Ibn Saud.

In fact, Britain had frustrated Arab ideas of independence perfectly legally, through Sir Henry McMahon's shrewd use of 'legalese'.

In his later letters to Hussein, McMahon paved the way for the Arab leader's downfall by making it clear that all issues now under discussion were 'subject to the approval of Britain's other ally in the region', an important legal technicality that first appears in writing only *after* the Arabs had already accepted Britain's offer of cash, arms and gold.

That other ally was, of course, France and this apparent deceit marks the moment when Arab frustration with the West begins, politics in the region split into pro- and anti-Western factions, and Iraq gradually moved towards the Communist camp.

Despite all his disappointments, Hussein still played an important part in Arab affairs, two of his sons being crowned king in two of the newly formed Arab kingdoms after the Great War: Abdullah in Transjordan and Feisal in Iraq.

Feisal had initially been proclaimed King of Syria in March 1920, but was removed by the French four months later on Bastille Day. The British, however, offered him the crown of Iraq instead and, after a plebiscite, Feisal was duly crowned in August 1921.

King Feisal was succeeded in 1933 by his only son, Ghazi, killed in a car crash in 1939. King Ghazi, in turn, was succeeded by his four-year-old son, King Feisal II, whose uncle Prince Abdul-Illah was to act as Regent until King Feisal's coronation in May 1953, the same day as his cousin, Hussein, officially became King of Jordan. Both were now eighteen years old.

Five years later, on 14 July 1958, King Feisal II and almost the entire Iraqi royal family were killed in the palace courtyard in a military coup, bringing to an end the Iraqi monarchy, parliament and constitution in one fell swoop.

Since the republican revolution, four Iraqi presidents have come and gone. General Kassem, the coup leader, was executed in 1963, succeeded by President Arif who met his end in a helicopter crash, paving the way for his brother, Arif Jr., who was overthrown in 1968 by General al-Bakr.

In 1979, President al-Bakr stood down in favour of Vice President Saddam Hussein, who invaded Iran the following year. The Iran-Iraq war finally came to an end in 1988 with huge casualties on both sides but, in August 1990, Saddam took on an easier target, Kuwait.

However, the following January, with the support of the UN Security Council, a coalition of British and US troops moved against the Iraqi forces, pushing them back across the border, whereupon President Bush declared a ceasefire.

UN sanctions against Iraq continued through the 1990s and, finally, after searches for weapons of mass destruction by UN weapons inspectors had been called off, President Bush Jr. and British premier Tony Blair took it upon themselves to invade Iraq in March 2003.

Defying the wishes of the UN Security Council, a British and US coalition force invaded Iraq and, after a short war, arrested President Saddam Hussein in December 2003. My elder brother, Saeed al-Hammashe, was chosen as the lead judge at his trial. It seemed to me that justice would now prevail, justice for every man, woman and child, justice even for Saddam himself. How could it not, with my elder brother at the helm? But to my horror and disbelief, within hours of his appointment, he had been stripped of his role by the same people who had stripped our country of its soul. The opportunity for our beloved homeland to unite through forgiveness was once again swept away from us. Saddam Hussein was executed on 30 December 2006.

Despite President Bush and Mr Blair's assurances, the violence in Iraq continues unabated to this day. The war goes on, my nation's despair must continue and, instead of elation, all I feel is pain.

What you seek you will never find, for when the Gods created Man, they let Death be his lot; eternal life they withheld.

Let your every day be full of joy; love the child that holds your hand; let your wife delight in your embrace, for these alone are the concerns of humanity.

– *The Epic of Gilgamish*, the world's first known writing, *circa* 4000 BC